LOST WORLD OF PATAGONIA

DANE HATCHELL

SEVERED PRESS
HOBART TASMANIA

LOST WORLD OF PATAGONIA

CHAPTER 1

Gerald Hawkins ran into Will Prescott's back, who had stumbled on a tree root. The thick foliage of the jungle slowed them at best to a trot. With the flying terror in hot pursuit, moving cautiously wasn't a smart action, to say the least. The terrain hindered a quick escape. The land rose and fell; sometimes the two ran up an incline of several feet only to descend farther on the other side.

"Watch your step, man! That thing's right behind us!" Gerald put a hand underneath Will's left arm and helped the man gain his footing. If they didn't make it back to the cave, the winged beast was sure to get them.

"We're not too far," Will said, labored. "We just have to cross that ridge. The cave's on the other side."

A branch bent under Will's hand and snapped back, hitting Gerald smack in the nose. *Fuck!* Tears welled in his eyes impairing his vision. Momentarily loss of vision was the least of his worries. Seeing the monster wouldn't aid him in any way to stop it. There were only two chances for survival. *One,* they both made it to the cave before turning to shredded meat by the monster's claws. Or *two,* the thing would only get one of them and be detained long enough for the other to make it to safety.

Will was in front. Gerald was in the rear. The odds were not on his side.

As the two climbed the ridge, he considered grabbing Will by the back of his clothing and send him tumbling down as an offering to the deadly pursuer.

"Do you hear that? It's the drone. Since our satellite phone's dead, Perkins must have sent the drone back to check on us."

"Whooptie shit! Shut up and move!" The goddamn drone wouldn't do them any good right now. Maybe if it had a Hellfire missile to launch, but that sure as fuck wasn't happening.

The two were close to the top of the ridge, *so close.* Gerald hoped God didn't have some sick sense of humor and pull the preverbal rug out from under them at the last second. He stole a moment to glance behind at the misty sky above. *Nothing*. It was too good to be true.

Will had just stepped to the top when Gerald lost his foothold, probably from turning his attention away from his path to look for the predator. "Shit! Will!" He landed flat on his stomach and began to slide down.

Without any hesitation, Will spun around and dropped to his knees, reaching down and grabbing Gerald by the hand.

Fear had Gerald's mind racing and a cold numbness gripping the back of his head. He felt lighter than air as copious amounts of adrenalin pumped throughout his body. Will had stopped his descent, and with a quick tug from his mate and his feet finding terra firma, Gerald scrambled to the top of the ridge.

"Hurry!" Will pushed Gerald in front of him.

The two made a mad dash to the cave opening a short distance away. The drone had made a safe landing on the flat area to the side of the cave.

The whooshing flap of wings invaded the air behind the two. An unholy cry followed, *SKEER-AK,* cutting like a knife ripping down the spinal column.

The flying monster hadn't abandoned its hunt after all. That son-of-a-bitch was just biding its time until it had a clear shot at the tasty meat morsels.

Sanctuary was so close. Gerald never desired anything more in his life than to reach it. He blocked everything but the cave's opening from his mind. Gerald was an Olympic runner, kicking into overdrive to win the race. He was running from a chasing tiger toward the edge of a low cliff above calm waters. Victory was only a few steps away!

Gerald lowered his head as if to break the ribbon across the finish line and skidded to a halt as he entered the cave's narrow opening. Safe at last!

The monster bird screeched again, but more horrifying than that, Will screamed out in ghastly pain.

Dropping to his knees, Gerald spun around and saw a horrified contortion on his companion's face he knew would haunt him the remainder of days. Two large, reptilian-like claws had a deadly grip on Will's shoulders. Blood gushed where thick black talons embedded into soft flesh.

Another paralyzing shriek sliced the air and echoed throughout the cave. Gerald felt his colon quiver, threatening to spill his bowel's contents.

In a lightning fast moment Will's feet left the ground, and he disappeared from sight.

The fading cries of his companion twisted the knife of dread buried in Gerald's gut. He closed his eyes and put his hands over his ears. The screams still reverberated in his head. They were so loud he realized it was his memory tormenting him, not the uncontrollable wails of a man agonizing in pain and in fear of an unimaginable death.

Gerald was alive. Alive! He had made it to safety. Only moments before he'd considered sacrificing Will in order to save his own hide. But it was Will who had saved him and gave him the chance to escape. Will's unselfish actions cost him his life.

Though he was glad he had survived, Gerald felt the heaviness of guilt weigh on him. It was only guilt, though. Harboring an ill emotion was much better than going through an excruciating death, shredded piece by piece by a flying beast that looked like the pterodactyls he saw on TV, watching *The Land of the Lost* on Saturday mornings as a kid.

He had seen it enough in the initial attack to be awestruck by its savage beauty. The upperparts were a deep, glossy brown. The breast was white and streaked with brown. The head had a triangular shape at the top, and its bill was long and flat, resembling crocodile jaws filled with sharp teeth. The irises of the eyes had a golden shine and looked cold and threatening. With a wingspan of what he guessed exceeded 30 feet, this modern dinosaur was far deadlier than any bird of prey in the outside world. And at this point, even if the drone had carried a Hellfire missile, he couldn't be sure it would have the power to kill the mighty dinosaur or just piss it off.

His pulse had pounded like a drum in his head for so long, Gerald began to notice it again as his heart rate slowly returned to normal. Safe. Sound. For the moment, at least.

What now? He still wore his backpack, which was loaded with the remainder of supplies for the trip back to Perkins, who waited at the truck. The hike back out would take more than a week, depending on the terrain, and what they hadn't considered before—the strange creatures in this remote land.

On the trip in, he and Will didn't see any sign of threatening indigenous life. If they had, they would have turned tail and run. Screw the mission. In fact, they hadn't seen much of any type of native life other than ordinary insects such as flies, no-see-ums, and beetles. A few times they caught sight of strange animals moving in the distance, but the creatures never stayed in view for long—always disappearing in the brush before they could get a good look at them. Which was okay by both of them. The last thing they wanted to do was worry about becoming a large ferocious cat's or beastly bear's dinner. Whatever animals lived in the region seemed to have a profound fear of man. Perhaps because he was a creature they were unfamiliar with.

That was then. This was now, and whatever alerted the pterodactyl to their presence, if fear of uncertainty had played a part, it certainly did no longer.

Gerald slowly removed the straps of his backpack off his shoulders and laid it on the cave's floor. He pulled out one of the last two bottles of water and took a conservative sip after twisting off the cap. Not much left to survive on very long. Searching for water might turn out to be the last thing he would ever do.

Again, what now? He grabbed the 9mm pistol from the holster. The slide was back, indicating it was empty. The pterodactyl had taken at least six direct hits from his gun. At first shot, the dinosaur had seemed startled by the discharge of the weapon, either from the gun blast or being hit by a lead projectile. When it returned for another swoop not long after he and Will decided to head for the cave, the gunshots did little to deter it. So whether he hit his target or not, in the end it made little difference. Maybe a direct headshot would work. Unfortunately, Gerald had expended two magazines on the flight back to the cave—sometimes shooting blindly up into the air in hopes of warding off the foe. The other two magazines on his belt were missing. They were somewhere between the cave and about half a mile back into the forest. *Fuck it.* It didn't matter much anyway.

Gerald inched his way to the cave opening and looked around. He saw a few black droplets on the ground where Will had been snatched away. To his right was the drone. His only connection to civilization. He'd have one chance to get help, and he didn't need to make any mistakes.

He went back into the cave and pulled a small notebook and pen from the backpack. Turning toward the light spilling in from the cave's mouth, he wrote.

'I'm in trouble. A large flying creature I can best describe as a dinosaur has killed Will. If I try to leave the cave I won't make it. Use the GPS and rescue me. Bring the best firepower you can. Not sure what we're up against.'

He put down the pen and notebook and rummaged through the backpack. His hand came back with a cloth pouch. Gerald opened it and fingered the contents, pulling out two unusual, beautiful uncut gemstones. This was his ticket out of here. Gemstones so rare the owner only had to name a price of their choosing.

One stone was larger than the other. He almost chose the larger one, but after a thought, placed it back into the bag. Picking up the pen and notebook, he continued to write.

'I'm including one of the smaller red diamonds just to prove we've hit the jackpot. Get in touch with Lear, tell him I have 500 million dollars in gemstones with me-and there're more to be found. He'll never see them if I'm not rescued.'

Would the note work? Gerald didn't want to beg and didn't want to threaten. He had to play the few cards he had just right. Appealing to Henry Lear's greed seemed to be the best bet in getting out alive. It would be too easy for the rich man to ignore Gerald's predicament and simply fund another expedition at a later time. A 500 million dollar carrot was sure, he hoped, to make Lear act immediately and get him the hell out of there.

Gerald tore the page from the notebook and folded it to the size of a credit card. Now the trick would be to put it in the drone along with the uncut gemstone without meeting a similar fate as Will.

Outside the cave, trees he knew only as *palms* fanned leafy arms among several other towering trees of the forests. He had read somewhere that there were over 16,000 species of trees in South America. The forest was a beautiful sight to behold. It had more of an appeal before Gerald had to fear what unknown might lurk within to kill him.

For now, everything was calm. Gerald inched his way toward the cave's opening until his head was completely out. Nothing. Again, the calm before the storm? Perhaps, but venturing outside would always be a chance. Hopefully, the pterodactyl was still busy with Will, giving Gerald enough time to complete his task. He paused for a second at the morbid reasoning. Still, it was the truth.

He cautiously stepped toward the drone. It was only a few yards away. His head turned like a gun turret on a tank, constantly watching the sky.

A few moments later he was by the drone's side. He stooped and fumbled open the small storage compartment. In went the note and the rough gemstone, and then he latched the compartment shut.

Gerald took a deep breath and looked about the sky a final time. *Please, let this work.* He almost made the sign of the cross, something his mother used to do after a small prayer, but stopped. Gerald was too intelligent to be superstitious.

His fingers found the tiny toggle switch on the fuselage. A green LED brightened as he threw the switch—the transponder now active.

He dashed back to the opening of the cave, lay flat on his stomach, and watched the drone.

Several minutes passed, not too long a time for Gerald to panic, but long enough that he felt incredible tension release as the engine came to life. The annoying buzz the drone made now sounded like a comforting lullaby.

Ouch! A sharp pain pierced his right calf muscle. He instinctually kicked his leg and felt something bump against it, right before a chunk of flesh ripped off.

Gerald flipped over and drew his legs toward his body. His hand immediately covered the bleeding calf. To his shock, a lizard about a foot in length stood on its hind legs and chewed away at the mouthful of Gerald's flesh.

What the hell? I hope that thing didn't poison me. Gerald was more concerned with bacteria associated with the reptile's mouth than the threat such a small animal presented. The lizard was just out of kicking range, and if it made one more step closer, he was going to punt it into tomorrow.

The drone's engine whine intensified. It was on its way and couldn't deliver the message too soon. The buzz of the engine faded as it made its takeoff and vacated the area.

Bastard. Gerald reached for the backpack. There were medical supplies in a kit, and he wanted to hurry and wipe the wound with alcohol to minimize the damage.

The lizard stepped to the side, snaking its head on a long neck.

This was the strangest lizard he'd ever seen. It continued to stand on its back legs, and now that Gerald paid closer attention, he saw why. Its front legs were too short for it to use as legs. In fact, they looked more like arms than legs. And though it was difficult to tell, he saw three fingered hands with tiny claws on the creature.

The lizard stepped one foot forward and stuck its head out chicken-like. The tail seemed to balance the brown and yellowish body as it moved.

"Stay back, or I'll turn you into a belt."

The warning went unheeded. The bipedal lizard rushed forward and bit Gerald's shoe.

In one swift motion, he grabbed the critter and tossed it as hard and as fast as he could. It hit the wall somewhere in the darkness beyond, letting out a tiny cry that sounded like someone had stepped on a dog's squeaky toy.

"Fuck you, little bastard." Gerald opened the backpack and pulled out the med-kit. He found a small square foil pouch and opened it. The alcohol soaked wipe stung as he cleaned the wound. It looked like the creature had taken a bigger bite than its mouth. Powerful jaws for one so tiny.

Next, he applied antibiotic ointment and covered that with an adhesive bandage. Gerald hoped that would do the trick.

If that lizard was still alive, it'd be back. Maybe even when he was asleep. That was something he couldn't stand for. Gerald wished he had some bullets left, but all he had was a knife.

Stabbing the thing might be hard to do. His best bet was to club it. Both his and Will's pick and shovel were still in the cave. Now was a good of time as any to play Whack-A-Mole, or in this case, *Whack-A-Lizard*.

His hand reached in the backpack and found a flashlight. He pointed it toward the rear of the cave and pushed the *on* switch.

The light came on illuminating a short distance before him, and just inside the darkness six pairs of glowing green embers hovered nearly a foot above the ground. It didn't take but a second for Gerald to realize the embers were eyes. Eyes reflecting the light of his flashlight. Not just one pair, but six. Now he had six little bastards to deal with.

As if sensing it was: *Advantage, lizard,* the lounge of lizards chicken-stepped toward Gerald.

A shovel leaned right inside the cave's opening. Gerald picked up the small tool. He pointed the shovel at the lizards and shook it at them as a warning.

The bipedal lizards waved their small arms about, opening and closing their clawed hands. One moved a step forward, then another three steps. From the looks of things, they weren't going to leave without a fight.

He brought the shovel down hard on the cave's floor a few feet from the lizards. The abrupt noise had them retreat a short distance, but only for a moment. Before Gerald had the chance to raise the shovel in defense again, one lizard bounded forth. He had just enough time to compose himself—bringing his hiking boot forward—and send the lizard back beyond its mates.

"Don't fuck with me." Gerald brandished the shovel before him, starting to believe he was going to win this war. They were just too small to put up much of challenge. He wondered if they would make a tasty meal later on. To the victor go the spoils.

A rustle in the far darkness gave Gerald pause. He extended his hand with the flashlight as far as it would go. Two large illuminated embers hovered a few feet above the ground.

"Shit...."

The damn things had a mother.

The hiss of the large lizard seemed to embolden her offspring. All six ran toward him at once. Some attacked his legs; some leaped and hit him in the chest.

Gerald swatted and kicked like a man attacked by a swarm of bumblebees. Clothing tore, flesh ripped, and blood started to fly. He had no choice but to backpedal his way to safety, out of the protection of the cave.

He grabbed one little beast that had embedded hand and foot claws into his chest. With lightning fast speed, he yanked the lizard from its stronghold, and hurled it into the rocky cave's exterior.

With two lizards feasting on his right leg, he still managed to bring his foot up and stomp a lizard gnawing on his left ankle. He could win this fight if he acted quickly—if he didn't lose too much blood.

The mother beast in the cave hissed again.

Gerald had to free himself of the minor distractions in order face her head to head.

Another stomp, another lizard down. One of the lizards hanging on his right leg fell off, and a boot came down on it too. Gerald grabbed the other still on his right leg and smashed it to the ground. The last lizard came from his peripheral. He managed to catch it in mid-air as it leaped for him.

The mother exited the cave, appearing as if she were about to jump the distance to Gerald, but hesitated—waving her arms and snaking her head on her long neck. Mother lizard was as big as a large dog. Her teeth were long and plentiful enough, Gerald feared, to take a man's arm or leg off.

Baby lizard squealed. At least for now, Gerald held a trump card.

"Stay back! Stay back, or I'll kill it." He felt stupid for talking to the reptile. This was not an ordinary reptile, though. The small size of the lizards in the cave created a deception. The mother painted a true picture of what he battled. These weren't some species of South American lizard. This was a carryover from prehistoric times. Just like the pterodactyl, this was some type dinosaur.

Gerald cautiously stepped back, looking for an escape. He might have a chance if he could climb a tree. There was only one way to find out.

A tree a few yards away had branches low enough for him to reach. If he timed things right, his plan just might work.

"I'm not going to hurt it. I'm going to give it right back." Gerald moved slow and steady toward the tree.

Mother dino matched him step for step. Keeping a few yards between them.

"Just a few more seconds, and I'll set it free."

The mother dinosaur hissed and raised her clawed hands into the air.

Gerald had pushed the standoff too far and had to move quickly. He lifted the baby dino into the air and let it drop, bringing his foot up like a punter on 4th and long. The small dinosaur sailed through the air and landed behind its mother.

Gerald dashed for the tree, careful to watch his footing along the way. He dared not waste a second to look behind him.

Just as he arrived at the base of the tree, fire shot into both of his shoulders. A horrific *SKEER-AK* chilled the air and distorted reality. Fearful dread washed down from the top of his head and rattled his bowels. Steel-like claws dug into flesh and around bone as Gerald's feet lifted off the ground.

The pterodactyl had returned to a known food source and was immediately rewarded.

The wind blew reptilian funk into Gerald's face as large brown wings flapped by his sides. The game was over. He'd lost. Substituting one inconceivable death for another.

The pain had grown in his shoulders to the point where it began to numb. "God, please," he sobbed. "Let me die right now. Take me now!" Gerald managed to make the sign of the cross, thinking his mother would be so pleased with him.

The pterodactyl's nest loomed in the distance. Three hungry mouths waited to be fed.

CHAPTER 2

Henry Lear stood behind an opulent mahogany desk in his study, his hands behind his back, rocking on the heels of shoes made of leather cured in baths of rye, oat flour, and yeast—hand-finished and soaked in wood liquor. A lazy stream of smoke rose from his 60-ring gauge cigar disappearing up to the 16-foot ceiling.

Perkins would arrive at any moment. If the news the man carried with him was genuine, Lear stood to triple his current worth of three hundred million dollars. That would make him, Henry H. Lear, a billionaire. One billion dollars. Truly an almost incomprehensible amount of money, in reality. Although the way the government wasted money, many have been desensitized to the value of one billion dollars. It's just *one* billion, right? How many billions made up the U.S.A.'s annual budget? Over three thousand billion.

How much money is too much for one person to have? He'd been asked that question more than once over the years by friends and enemies alike. In his early years, after acquiring more money than any normal personal could spend in ten lifetimes, something shifted inside his psyche. Perhaps it was self-preservation because having all that money sucked his desire to achieve in life right out of him. At the time, he thought of the story of Alexander the Great, who cried after a battle, realizing there were no other lands to conquer—he had defeated them all.

Henry needed a goal—a vision if you will. A point he must strive for. He remembered daydreaming in church one Sunday morning, a weekly event he hated, but was forced to attend by his parents. As he fidgeted on the thin cushion on the oak pews, the preacher's voice cut through the fog of his insignificant musings. The preacher read: "Without vision, the people will perish." For some reason that message stuck with him the rest of his life thus far, regardless of the original context the preacher meant.

It was true. Henry needed a vision to keep pushing forward. And now that all the women, cars, houses, and drugs weren't enough to motivate him, becoming a billionaire was. On occasion, he worried what would happen to him if he did achieve his goal. Would he again find life without savor? Something inside told him *no*. He needed to earn that billion—achieve that status. From there, as if he would ascend to a higher plane of spiritual knowing, the rest of his life would become clear. Then his life would head in a direction he was totally unable to fathom now.

A voice came over speakers built into massive bookshelves behind him: "Mr. Lear, Ronald Perkins has arrived."

"Excellent. Please have Mr. Perkins escorted in."

"Yes, sir."

Henry drew in on the cigar and tasted the mild fruit and toasted nut notes from the blended tobaccos. As strange as it seemed, he couldn't remember the last time he had been so excited to meet someone. He certainly felt less as he waited to meet the current President of the United States. In public, businessmen are made the bane of society's ills by politicians, accused of stealing from the hard working common man. It was the Politicians who really robbed the poor populist blind. Creating government programs for the main purpose of helping themselves get reelected, while having to borrow more money than the country collected in taxes to pay for them. Years of undisciplined spending had infected the economy with a hidden virus—taxes and inflation that did nothing but lower the standards of living across the country. It was the politicians who were destroying the United States, not the businessmen.

A knock came from the door.

"Come in." Henry turned and walked to the side of his chair, his thigh touched against the desktop. He latched both his thumbs and forefingers to either side of the lapels of his jacket, resting his arms against his side. His nose turned slightly in the air. His gaze narrow and eyelids half open. While going to dinner one night, a girlfriend of his once told him he looked stupid when he stood like that—especially with that huge cigar shoved between his lips. He had his driver pull to the side of the road right then and put her ass out on the side of the Santa Monica Freeway. That was the last time he had seen or heard from her.

The double doors opened, and two young men who could have played linebackers for the Dallas Cowboys followed behind Ronald Perkins. Once inside the doors, the two escorts flanked to opposite sides and stood at attention—their hands crossed by their belt buckles.

Perkins' mouth slightly dropped open as he moved his gaze around the room. He stopped a few feet from Lear's desk, briefly looked behind him as if checking to see if his escorts were there, and then fixed his attention to the man behind the desk.

Henry removed the cigar from his mouth and held it to the side. "Mr. Perkins, please take a seat." He diverted his attention to the back. "You gentleman may leave."

Perkins had only one choice where it came to sit—a leather chair off to one side of the desk. He stepped toward the chair as the double doors closed with the bright snap of the doorknob's latch bolt finding the slot in the strike. Arriving at the chair, he hesitated and looked back at Lear. "Uh, I didn't change clothes. They're a few days old."

"No matter. If we can't clean the stench off I can always buy another chair. Sit." Henry maneuvered his chair and sat, swiveling over to face Perkins, who now was seated.

"I washed up on the jet, but I didn't have any clean clothes to put on. Your men met me right as I entered town and took everything I had—even my cellphone."

"Not everything, right, Mr. Perkins?" Henry rapped the cigar on the side of a crystal ashtray on his desk, knocking off the lengthening ash.

"No, I guess not. Not everything." Perkins nervously tapped his left foot on the hardwood floor.

Henry relaxed his shoulders and sat straighter in his chair. "And that's why I had you sent here, directly to meet with me. I wanted to deal with you personally—so that we may build a trust. Don't worry about the things my men took from you. I'm going to make up for that and reward you in ways you've never dreamed. Before we begin, can I have something brought in for you to drink? Water, coffee, or perhaps something a bit stronger?"

"No, no thank you." Perkins wiggled in his chair, his eyes bright and hopeful.

"Very well, may I see what you have for me?"

"Yes, sir!" Perkins' hand reached into his jacket pocket and removed a pouch. He eagerly leaned over and placed it in Lear's outstretched hand.

Henry brought the pouch under his eyes and gazed at it for a moment. He set the pouch on the desk and slowly pulled at the string to widen the opening. Once in view, he felt air deflate from his tightened chest. It was a genuine red diamond—the largest ever discovered. "It's absolutely magnificent."

"Yeah. It doesn't even look real, does it?"

"At over six hundred carats, I do see your point. But it is real." Henry placed a finger and gently ran it along the smooth and curved surfaces. Then, he carefully moved the stone aside and opened a desk drawer. His hand went in and came out with a bound stack of 100-dollar bills. He placed it on the desk, and then reached in for another, and another, and then another—stacking them side by side.

"And that's not the biggest one, according to Hawkins. He said so in a note." Perkins leaned forward in the chair, hands gripping the armrest.

"Yes. Yes, I've been informed about the note. What do you make of it? Attacked by a flying dinosaur? Do you think Hawkins was sane when he wrote that? Perhaps suffering from a fever?"

"I knew Gerald well enough that I don't think he was bullshitting. I don't know why he would do that anyway. As far as his mental state, the note seemed rational enough. One thing for sure, he was in right mind enough to put the note and the gem on the drone."

"So you're telling me you didn't see the video footage the drone took when it left the cave?"

"Footage? No…uh, didn't take the time. No, sir, after I read the note, I called in the report and hightailed it out of there."

Two more stacks of 100s came up from the drawer and were placed next to the others. Henry scratched his chin. "Were you aware that the drone's camera is connected to a satellite link? It has the ability to send real-time images anywhere in the world, specifically to me."

"Uh…no, sir. I didn't know."

"Oh yes. It's quite a sophisticated piece of machinery. Why, it even told us you connected your phone to its video. You must have forgotten, Mr. Perkins, but you *have* downloaded the video on your phone." He placed two more bundled stacks of 100s from the drawer on the desk.

"Look—I don't know. I must have had the app on to automatically download. The video might have been on my phone. But I haven't seen it."

"Really? Because we found a few still shots cut from the video on your phone. The same ones that you sent to a newspaper. How did that happen?"

Perkins abruptly stood from his chair, his body trembled, his arms and hands wide apart. "I'm sorry, Mr. Lear. Honestly! I wasn't thinking. They…they probably won't even believe they're real."

"Have you spoken with anyone at the newspaper? Do they know who you are? Who you work for?"

"No! Not at all. I set up a special email account to deal with them. I used a false name, and we were working on a deal but were nowhere close to finishing it."

"So the location and the secret are safe? Do you promise me that? I have to know the truth."

Voice quivering, Perkins said, "No one knows! I swear on my life. I was just trying to sell the pictures for some extra money."

Henry stared long and hard while Perkins looked like he was going to shiver out of his skin. Very mildly, Henry said, "I believe you, Mr. Perkins."

Perkins closed his eyes and sighed. "Thank you. I'm so sorry I did that. I was stupid. Stupid!"

"Yes. But you have confessed your sins, and now you shall reap your reward." Henry reached in the same desk drawer from where he had removed the money and came up with a black 9mm pistol with a suppressor on the end.

Perkin's expression turned to shock, and before he could plead for forgiveness, Lear fired the pistol. The bullet hit the man right in the heart. He dropped to his knees, gasping for air, and clutching at the wound. His wide eyes looked off into the distance, and his last breath escaped his lips.

"Ms. Sanders, please send someone in to clean up," Henry spoke into the air.

"Yes sir, Mr. Lear. Right away."

Having his enemies killed had always brought him great pleasure. Now that he personally participated, his pleasure had exponentially increased.

***

Something shifted in Gerald's oblivion, emerging consciousness like a slowly rising crescendo. Awareness grew from discordant thoughts and sharpened as his senses kicked in. Wind rustled through tree leaves. The earth felt warm and sticky-moist on his exposed arms. A dull pain in his head preceded other aches and throbs waking throughout his body.

His eyes opened in short blinks, drinking in the beauty of the savage land. The lush green foliage hid him like a small insect in tall, thick grass.

He was alive. Hurt, no doubt, but alive. Death had been so close—as before, but fear had energized him at the last possible minute and gave him one last chance. He remembered:

Although he thought his strength had been sapped by the strong talons of the pterodactyl, seeing her hungry hatchlings forced mind over matter. He managed a futile effort to pull its claws out of his left shoulder and failed. Then he remembered the six-inch knife tucked securely away in its sheath attached to his belt.

Gerald fumbled the flap aside and grabbed the plastic handle. With as much strength as he could muster, and as rapidly as possible, he repeatedly stabbed the clawed foot. To his surprise and elation, the flying reptile squawked and let go of his left shoulder. He immediately switched the knife to the other hand and franticly stabbed away at its right claw.

The pterodactyl held firm, shifting her flight pattern away from her nest, flying erratically.

Damn it, let go! Gerald now considered the dinosaur might skip feeding him to her children and bring him to the ground where she would dine.

SKEER-AK!

The pterodactyl's cry didn't come from his attacker. Gerald turned his head up and saw another winged reptile willing to join the fray to fight for the prize. The pterodactyl that held him saw the interloper too. It screeched in defiance and quickened the flap of its wings.

During the distraction, Gerald put all of his power into one last jab. The blade went in almost half the length. He then gave the handle a twist, tearing deeply into flesh.

Talons loosening from his shoulder brought instant relief. He saw his attacker meet the intruder in mid-air amidst warning cries and brandished talons ripping the space between them.

He plunged through tree branches and leaves, slowing his descent, but getting poked, scraped, and cut along the way. Then, darkness swallowed him whole.

There was no way to know who won the battle or by what miracle the victor didn't return for its reward. The fact that no other creature in this remote land had made a meal of him was surprising enough. What else hid among this unknown land?

With his senses back online and working together again, the picture of his health slowly developed. He was sore but didn't seem to have any major lacerations other than the claw marks, although he was scraped and cut. His body had to have sustained deep bruises. After sitting up and going through several arm and leg motions, along with wiggling fingers and toes, nothing appeared to be broken. Another miracle.

Another miracle. Maybe his mother was right about everything she believed about God. Gerald turned his gaze toward the sky. "Thank you." The act seemed silly on one level but fit the moment.

How long had he been unconscious? Dirt stained the face of his watch. He wiped it off, and it revealed it was around 16 hours from the last time he remembered. His stomach told him it had been a while since he had eaten, and his mouth was so dry his tongue couldn't find any moisture. There was plenty of water in the area, in small streams and bogs. The problem lay in the microorganisms contained in the water. Without water purification tablets, he risked intestinal parasites along with a host of other woes. Gerald's supply of tablets waited in his backpack at the cave.

At or near the cave is where his rescuers would try to find him. As much as he hated the idea, Gerald knew his only hope of surviving was to find his way back to the cave area and wait.

How far away was the cave? He had no way of knowing. Gerald went into shock almost from the moment the flying reptile snatched him away. The time in its grasp, which seemed like an eternity, probably hadn't been long.

He reached in his side pocket and pulled out a compass. The needle rocked a bit on its pivot and pointed toward the north. With any luck he'd be able to find his way back. He didn't know if mama dinosaur took refuge back in the cave, and he really didn't want to find out. Now he hoped he could make it to the area, this time taking shelter in a tree. The strange fruits he and Will occasionally came upon on the trek might very well dictate life or death. In order to live, he had to hydrate. If the juice from the fruits weren't enough—or made him ill—he'd have to chance the water or gamble on going back into the cave for the purification tablets.

Once up on wobbly legs, a dull pain eased throughout his left knee. Perhaps his leg had twisted a bit as the branches cushioned his descent. The pain might slow him down but wasn't enough to stop him. Gerald steadied his hand holding the compass and gazed toward the southeast. Time to move before night fell.

*

Gerald's lips slightly stung from the citrusy fruit he had found and ate an hour prior. It had tasted like a cross between a grapefruit and an orange, with a slight hint of kiwi. It wasn't sweet, and it wasn't sour, and only slightly bitter. He realized such primitive fruit didn't have the benefit from years of man's cultivation to produce a more savory product. So far, his body had accepted it without the slightest hint of rejection. Which was great news, since he had picked two others to enjoy later—if they proved to be safe.

The sun had just started to breach the horizon. No matter, the cave was in sight from his vantage point. It was time to find a comfortable tree to spend the night.

Gerald looked around, and there were a minimal amount of trees suitable for climbing—most had lower branches still some 20 feet above the ground.

Something bustled in the tall grass, rolling through it like a bowling ball. At first Gerald froze—afraid if he moved he'd be detected, or if he didn't move in the right direction—he'd end up in the same boat.

Just as he picked a direction to scamper, an odd-looking beast broke into a narrow clearing, heading slightly away from him. That was a relief! The animal wasn't coming after him.

The creature was around 3 feet long and most resembled a modern pig, but the body had skin more like a hippo or elephant. In fact, its face looked more like an elephant except with much smaller ears and a short snout. One thing for sure, the animal was in a hurry.

It only took a moment for Gerald to discover why. Coming fast in his direction, two bodies near 8 feet in height cut through the foliage. As soon as the two spotted Gerald, their pursuit of the small animal ended.

"Holy shit." Any cherished musing he had earlier of a caring and benevolent God vanished.

Two dinosaurs looking like larger cousins to the previous batch of cave lizards stared curiously at Gerald. They, too, were bipedal, with legs that looked strong, and a tail nearly as long as the length of body and neck. Their heads turned from side to side, with eyes like obsidian marbles peering intently. In a way they almost looked cartoonish because of the false smile the sharp exposed teeth formed across the mouth. The bellies were matte white and the skin had marks in a bronze and tan pattern much like a copperhead snake.

The curiosity of the dinosaurs was the only thing keeping Gerald alive for the moment. In a Disney movie it would be a perfect time for the creatures to break out in a joyful song and dance. But as seconds quickly passed, it was beginning to look more like a scene from *Jurassic Park*. Where the Velociraptors show up for fun and games and end up staying for dinner.

Gerald may have fallen from the frying pan into the fire, but with nothing left to lose, he wasn't going down without a fight. He raised his arms in a wide arc, and yelled, "Hah!" He didn't stick around to see if his aggressive act was enough to scare the beasts away. A tree several yards ahead had branches within his reach, and Gerald never remembered reading anywhere that dinosaurs had the ability to climb.

The race was on.

He dashed toward the tree—pushing past the pain in his knee, his elbows chugging like the main rod connected to the wheels of a steam locomotive. Tall grasses slapped against his body, impeding his flight to safety. Gerald gave it all he had; he sucked in and heaved out air in his lungs.

As if pissed that the prey dared attempt an escape, the two creatures' uttered reptilian cries several syllables long. Each had its own distinct tone, lacing threatening hisses between ferocious warnings.

The dinosaurs hadn't hesitated for long. Gerald heard each clawed foot strike the earth and tear through the grass behind him. They were gaining—fast.

He stepped to the side to avoid a tree whose branches were too tall for him reach. It was as if he could feel the creatures' hot breaths on the back of his neck.

A broken tree branch on the ground nearly five feet long looked promising as a weapon. Gerald stooped and picked it up, and then turned to make a final stand.

Out of wild fear and pure luck, he jabbed it toward the nearest dinosaur and struck it in the face—and in one of its eyes.

It stopped cold in its tracks and let out an enraged yell. The other stopped as well, clawing at the air and jutting its head back and forth, as if waiting for the proper moment to strike.

It wasn't much of a defense, but it was all he had. There was no way he could win a fight, and he knew better than to believe the intruders would eventually tire and go away. The million-dollar question: Could he hold up long enough to make it up a tree?

The unhurt dinosaur stepped away from his companion, drawing Gerald's attention. It moved almost 180 degrees from the other, exposing his rear. This was not good. He slowly backed up, poking the stick toward the dinosaurs.

The injured creature got back into the game, snaking his head forward, and biting the air a few feet from Gerald's head. He turned and poked the stick at it, and then hurriedly turned to the other side and jabbed at the other. But the dinosaur moved quickly and in close enough to bite the stick—tearing it from Gerald's grasp. He raised his arm in a futile attempt to hold it back, but the creature wasted no time and bit Gerald up to the elbow of his right arm. The other attacked from behind, and as Gerald instinctually raised his other arm to ward off the foe, it bit his left forearm.

He was caught in the worst trap imaginable. Gerald pulled his right arm with all he had. He felt it loosen from the dino's grip. But with the dinosaur's teeth firmly embedded in the arm, skin and meat tore away, exposing bloody bone nearly to his wrist. Scalding fire from frayed nerves had him screaming uncontrollably.

The dinosaur biting the other arm pulled Gerald toward it in a tug-of-war match with its companion. The contest ended when it used a rapid jerk motion of its head and neck to snap the arm off at the elbow.

Gerald tumbled to the ground, blood spilling from the stump—splattering crimson on tall green grasses.

While one dinosaur devoured his left arm, the other mashed a three-clawed foot onto his chest. Thick nails gripped tightly while the dinosaur pulled its prize—the remaining part of his right arm—free from Gerald's shoulder.

Shock had Gerald's head buzzing. The time-forgotten creatures tore him apart like vultures scavenging carrion off the side of the road.

A foot caught him across the stomach, tearing a deep gash down to his thigh, catching intestines along the way, and pulling them outside the cavity. Then the attacker bit down on his leg, and the two dinosaurs divided the spoils of the hunt.

Gerald heard his mother's soothing voice, felt her warm embrace, and died wearing a euphoric smile across his face.

CHAPTER 3

Alex Klasse sat at his kitchen table, with a phone receiver pressed to his ear. He shifted his weight to the other ass cheek, wishing he had a landline in the living room where he could sit on a comfortable couch cushion and not a wooden ladderback chair. If he'd been allowed to use his cellphone, he could have given the interview from any room in his house—anyplace, anywhere actually.

But, noooooo. Art Corey, the host of the late night radio show *Shore to Shore, U.S.A.*, demanded landlines—for reception's sake. During the next break, Alex decided he would get up and get a pillow to sit on.

He'd get up now while Art interviewed the *famous* remote viewer Fred Danes, but was afraid Art might ask Danes about Klasse's work, something Art had indicated to Alex he might do, and Alex didn't want to miss that. But, noooooo, not one question about him and his work.

So far, Danes was on one of his prophetic, or perhaps better said, *pathetic*, diatribes of doom and gloom. Something about a new comet being discovered next year named Rubin-Sagan heading for Earth.

The interview droned on in Alex's ear:

"So, Fred. You're saying the comet won't actually hit the Earth, but fragments of it will peel off and become a meteor shower. How large of a shower are we talking about? Enough to become a planet killer or turn us back to the Stone Age?"

"The shower will be small enough that it does little damage to the Earth. But before you find any comfort in that, the meteors harbor bacteria harmful to plant life. Art, I'm talking all plant life. Every green thing on this planet will become infected…and die."

"Unbelievable. Crops? Trees? Grass? Everything we need to survive?"

"Yes. And it's not by some random chance. The bacteria has been engineered by aliens to kill us. Man has become a blight to this planet, and they want to wipe us out as a race before we infect the rest of the universe."

"Is there any chance we can avoid this? Any way we can prepare ourselves to save our planet from dying?"

Damn, Art sounds really upset, Alex thought. And for a moment he felt his heart plunge into his gut at the thought that something like this would actually happen.

"No, Art. There's nothing we can do. We're all dead. *Kaput. Nada.* Game over."

"Well. I…that's such a terrible thought, I don't know what to say."

"There is nothing to say, Art. It's time to bend over and kiss your ass goodbye."

"We're, uh, we're coming to the bottom of the hour. Thanks, Fred, for your time."

"You're welcome, Art. Until next time," Fred said, and ended the call.

Art shifted the tone and cadence in his voice as he continued, "Friends, I'd like to introduce a new sponsor to Shore to Shore, Just Cut Flowers. Just Cut Flowers is your online source for the freshest flowers available. Flowers can brighten anyone's day, and you don't need a special occasion to order. Just Cut Flowers, it's just what you need to give today. Call—"

Better call now before the alien bacteria kills them all. Alex laughed at the thought while he un-assed himself from the chair, and then headed for the bathroom. The break would last a good seven minutes.

What a crock of shit. Why did Art Corey have nut-jobs like this on his show? It couldn't be good for business. Why buy fucking flowers today when the Earth dies tomorrow? He unzipped his fly and let the accumulation of a half pot of coffee stream into the toilet. Why buy anything if it all ends soon? What difference would it make? We're all going to die. Fuck it and everything else too.

Alex was not the loyalist of listeners to Shore to Shore, but it was the leading radio talk show not afraid to step outside of accepted science. As a zoologist, his chosen profession, he'd have no reason to be invited on this show. But as a Cryptozoologist, his passion, it was a shoe made to custom fit.

Finishing his business, he zipped up, washed his hands, grabbed a couch pillow out of the living room, poured a cup of coffee, and sat back down at the table, pillow now cushioning his behind.

He put the phone receiver to his ear, and as he lifted the cup of coffee to his lips, a voice spoke.

"Mr. Klasse? You're on in sixty seconds," the show producer said.

"Thank you. I'm ready." The cup went back up for one quick taste before the interview began. This was it, *show time*. Now that the interview was here, his heart beat faster. That's the kind of man Alex was, a situation wasn't real until it became real. He didn't worry about future matters like some, who even made upcoming events worse by stressing out over them. Butterflies bumped his stomach's insides as Art's voice came over the phone.

"Welcome back to Shore to Shore. Our next guest, Alex Klasse, is an author and a professor of zoology at the Southwood University in Sarasota, Florida. Mr. Klasse is also known as one of the foremost experts in Cryptozoology. His interest in Cryptozoology ignited at the young age of ten when he saw what he believed to be a Skunk Ape in the Florida Everglades while on a hunting trip with his uncle. Mr. Klasse, good morning."

"A good morning to you, Art. And please, just call me Alex."

"Alex, before we dive into you latest book, *Cryptids in Your Backyard*, I wanted to get your thoughts of the pterodactyl photos printed in *The International Enquire*. Is it possible that dinosaurs still exist on Earth today?"

"I don't want to distract from your question, Art, but I would like to point out a pterodactyl is not a dinosaur. A pterodactyl is a genus of pterosaur with only one known species. Pterosaurs were winged flying reptiles."

"Oh, I didn't know that."

"Well, popular culture has the tendency to throw all prehistoric animals in the same bowl and call them dinosaurs. The subject is a bit complicated, but fascinating, and perhaps we can do a show on that one day. Getting back to the photos of the pterosaur, you'd have to agree anything appearing in *International Enquire* deserves extra scrutiny."

"That it would. But the publication has proved itself to be reputable, too."

"It has. So, when I first learned of the story and viewed the photos, I immediately thought it was some CGI pulled off by a movie studio. I found some high-resolution images on the internet and ran them through graphic software on my computer. Long story short, I stepped away at the end of the day believing the percentage for them being genuine was higher than them being a fake."

"Fascinating."

Alex gently cleared his throat. "Yes, the caveat is whoever sent those images in to the *Enquirer* is unknown, as well as when and where they were taken."

"If you learned of the location would you go there?"

Alex laughed. "Yes, if somebody'd fund me. Of course, there'd be so many others getting in on the action we'd be stepping on one another."

"No doubt. Now, tell us a little something about the new book."

Alex grabbed a furtive sip of coffee, settled into the chair, and continued the two-hour interview.

CHAPTER 4

Natasha Kamdar had most of her bags packed and waiting just inside her apartment door, ready to grab and run. The expedition would go out any day now, the final arrangements nearly complete. She was told to pack clothing of sturdy construction, something comfortable with fashion not in mind.

The climate varied in the remote location by as much as 100 degrees. This was because the vast area in Patagonia, South America, had mountains surrounding every side—essentially walling it off from the rest of the world. The area did contain one semi-active volcano, but because no human had ever ventured in for studies, nothing was known about it. Without the invention of satellites, no one would even know the volcano was there.

The mountains were cold and icy. But the Earth's molten magma so close to the land's surface heated the hundreds of miles of square acres hidden by the high mountain ranges. The heat rose from the land and mixed with the frigid, moist air high above, essentially shrouding the vast area in shielding mist.

I can't believe this is really happening, she thought as she lifted a 20-pound bag of rice and stacked it on top of another. It was Saturday morning at Sarasota Second Harvest Food Bank. Natasha and her crew had less than an hour remaining on their shift. Afterward, she had planned to do some last minute shopping. There were a few feminine products she didn't want to run short of—who knew if something would delay the return home? Three weeks was a long time anyway. There were just some modern amenities she wanted an ample supply of.

Is there something to this story? Do dinosaurs still live hidden somewhere on the Earth? There was only one way to find out, and that was for someone to go and explore firsthand. At least one corporation believed there was truth in the story. When Professor Klasse told her a rep from Ace Corporation called after his appearance on the radio show *Shore to Shore* and claimed to know where the pterosaur photos had been taken, and the corporation wanted to fund the expedition with him in the lead, she thought it was all bullshit concocted by some nut who listened to that late night garbage. But when the check arrived at the university in the form of a grant, she quickly changed her mind. *Money talks and bullshit walks*. Natasha smiled to herself. The phrase had become one of her father's favorites after learning the meaning of the regional adage. Born and raised in Jaipur, India, the American common language presented many barriers to his understanding of formal English. She still didn't think her father understood what it meant for a bride to get *cold feet* before her wedding.

Natasha lifted another bag of rice off the dwindling pile on the pallet and heaved it up over her head.

"Let me get that for you."

Smooth hands with slim fingers reached from behind and lifted the bag from her grasp. Matt King had jumped to her aid—again. She appreciated the concern, but being a woman wasn't a handicap, and she could have handled the bag just fine.

"Thanks, but I could have done that on my own." She had to choose her words properly, holding back a less respectful response. After all, Matt was an associate professor in zoology at the university, working with and in place of Professor Klasse sometimes. He was her teacher as well as the friend he tried to present himself to be. And with graduate school starting next year, she needed a certain *space* between them in their relationship. Not that there was anything unseemly about Matt, his personality, or his looks. He was in his early thirties and boyishly handsome. Natasha didn't want to give Matt the wrong idea, and she didn't want to make a certain *someone* jealous.

"I know, but I was right here, and I didn't want you to strain yourself." Matt placed the bag on top of the others, patting it smooth to receive the next one.

"You can help me over here with the fifty pound sacks of flour." Logan Sandler held a sack waist high, using his right hip to help push it up onto the shelf on the opposite wall.

Logan wasn't the tallest guy in the world, reaching a bit over 5'5", but he never let his stature dictate limitations in life. Natasha had never met such a focused person.

Sweat moistened Logan's brow, curling the sandy-blond hair across his forehead more than normal.

"What, afraid you're going to ruin your manicure? Looks like you're managing just fine," Matt said as he reached over and picked up the last bag of rice from the pallet.

"Oh, I'm more than capable. I just thought you might want put in a harder workout. You know, bulk up those scrawny biceps. I take every opportunity to keep myself fit. Walk instead of drive. Take stairs instead of the elevator, and at least two times a week go to clubs and dance my ass off."

"Your ass is still there. I can see it from up here," a voice said from above.

All heads turned.

"I was wondering where you wandered off too. What are you doing up there?" Natasha asked.

"You know me. I like to get multiple views on life. If I looked at things only from one plane, I'd be just another sheep grazing in the field. That's why football coaches are on the field and up in the stands. See, I did learn something valuable from playing high school football." Ben Wilson peered down from atop the row of shelves above his zoology associates. He wore a tee shirt with the sleeves crudely cut to the shoulders. Sweat glistened from ebony arms sculpted from countless hours in the gym. The shirt fit tightly enough to outline his washboard abs.

"Hey, Superman, why don't you come down here and put that hot bod of yours to work," Logan said, taking a moment to flex built tension from his shoulders.

"I'm not Superman. I'm the Beast," Ben said.

"The Beast, really?" Logan said.

"Yeah. The Beast was my favorite X-Man. You know, he was super smart, strong, and agile. When I was young, I didn't like school or reading or anything. I wasted a lot of time playing video games and watching cartoons. One day, I was at my aunt's house and found a stack of my cousin's old X-Men comics. I started looking at the pictures, and then I started reading. I was hooked instantly. After that, I spent my free time with studies and sports, sneaking in a little X-Men time along the way. Now, here I am. I'm the Beast."

"If I had to pick which of the X-Men I'd like to be, I'd be Rogue. I just love me some Anna Paquin," Logan said.

"You're not a girl, so you can't be Rogue. Besides, I'm picking Rogue," Natasha said.

Logan frowned. "Okay, then. I'll be Northstar—he has superhuman stamina, you know."

"Matt, how about you?" Ben asked.

Matt rolled his eyes. "Eh? Not really into superheroes. I'd don't think I'd look very good in yellow Spandex."

The whine of an electric forklift rose as the machine turned down the aisle and headed toward the group.

"Look, it's Professor X," Ben said, and laughed.

"At least our Professor X has hair," Logan said.

"Crap, more stuff to unload. I thought this was the last of it." Natasha crossed her arms and shifted her weight to her left foot. "I'm ready to go shopping for a few things before we leave."

Professor Klasse carefully maneuvered the forklift past his mates and in front of an empty shelf.

Natasha couldn't tell if the hardhat on his head cocked to one side was a fashion statement or if it had been bumped out of place. Either way, it complemented his looks well. Alex Klasse was twice her age, and that fact didn't make him look any less attractive.

Alex set the pallet of sugar on the floor and turned off the forklift. "Last one. We've put in a good day. I hope there're enough volunteers to take up our slack while we're away."

Ben grabbed onto the shelves' framework and quickly stepped his way down as if it were second nature.

Alex opened his mouth, perhaps to admonish a warning, but held his words before they came out. He just stared until Ben's shoes hit the floor, and the young man approached him.

"What?" Ben asked, obviously feeling the gaze of his Professor.

"I can't believe you did that," Alex said. "You could have hurt yourself."

"I know what I'm doing. My girlfriend back in high school was a gymnast. I used to practice with her back then. I do a little indoor rock climbing too. No worries," Ben said.

"Okay, I guess I shouldn't treat you like a kid. But I will be responsible for you—all of you—on the trip to South America. I honestly don't know what to expect. It could all prove to be some grand waste of time. Someone could get hurt—break a bone or fall. There will, more than likely, not be any dinosaurs for us to find. But I do expect a region that has been this isolated over this many centuries to have species of animals totally unique to anywhere else. Just like the two thousand and nine Son Doong Cave discovery in Vietnam. The animal life we find in Patagonia is potentially dangerous. We must keep our wits about, and safety is our number one priority."

"We know, Professor Klasse. You told us this several times now. We all know what to expect and what you expect from us." Matt reached over and placed his hand on Alex's shoulder.

Alex turned his attention back to Ben. "What did you mean when you said, 'Look, it's Professor X?' "

"You heard that? Damn, you have good ears. It wasn't anything, really. I said my favorite X-Man was the Beast, and the others picked who they wanted to be."

Alex grinned. The wrinkles on the sides of his eyes increased, making him look wiser. "I'd take a forklift over a wheelchair any day."

Professor Klasse turned the forklift's key and shifted into reverse, and over the annoying backup beep, he said, "To me, my X-Men."

After a few moments of blank stares showing his way, he said, "When I was a boy, I used to read the X-Men comics from the early sixties. 'To me, my X-Men,' was Professor X's battle cry to assemble his band of teenaged mutants." He released the brake, and the forklift moved backward.

Natasha saw what Alex did there, and she appreciated that he bridged the gap between the generations when appropriate. She was sure it was a tough job, no different than a parent-child relationship where you have to limit friendship so as not to diminish your authority. And if a professor at a university became too close a friend with his students, it invited a ton of complications for those involved. Complications of which she was well aware. Complications that seemed to weigh on her every waking minute of late.

"Let's get this over with." Natasha pulled a box cutter from her pocket and extended the blade.

Matt raised a hand. "We've got this, Natasha. You said you wanted to get some shopping in, so go ahead."

"Yeah, between me and the Beast here, we'll wrap things up in no time." Logan stepped up and pulled at the plastic wrap securing the stack of sugar. It stretched a bit, but didn't tear, so he reached an open hand out to Natasha.

"Really, you don't mind?" she asked.

"Nah, just go," Ben said.

"Thanks. I guess I'll see you guys when we get the call." She handed Logan the box cutter and headed to lockers in the break room.

Logan carefully sliced the layers of plastic, avoiding cutting into the sugar's protective bag. "Y'all packed up and ready to go? It's been awhile since I've been camping. I was in the Boy Scouts. My biggest concern is not having enough clean underwear."

"I'm ready. I had to sacrifice a few things to have room for my nutritional supplements. I hope the TSA doesn't go ape-shit and want me to throw them away. I've never flown before, and I'm not sure of all the rules. Seems like I read every other day the rules change." Ben picked up two sacks of sugar and placed them on a shelf.

"You're okay as long as the stuff isn't in your carry-on. Be careful, though, with aerosols. Pressure changes can cause them to leak," Matt said, while joining in on the work.

"Yep. I just bought a new tube of hair mousse. I usually buy pressurized mousse in a can. The last time I flew it leaked all inside my luggage. When I opened it, it looked like somebody had *jizzed* all over my stuff."

Ben laughed, and Matt grunted as he placed down his load.

Matt brushed his hands together, knocking off stray grains of sugar. "Logan, I finished reading the research paper you did for me. I forgot to thank you earlier. Sorry for that, but thank you—so much."

Logan stopped working and rubbed his hands free of sugar. He slightly turned his head, and his lips curled a shy smile. "You're welcome, Matt. I actually had fun doing it. You know you can always count on me."

"The semester's over. What's up with a research paper?" Ben asked, still lugging sacks.

Matt picked up another load. "I'm working on my PhD. Logan volunteered to help me continue my research without interruption while I was busy compiling final grades. My plan is to submit my thesis by the end of the year."

Ben turned to Logan. "What kind of research?"

"Emerging fungal pathogens and their effect on amphibians. There have been a lot of independent studies all over the world. I collected all the data, compared test results where experiments were duplicated, and added unique data. Pretty scary stuff, actually."

"Yeah, I've read about chytridiomycosis. If something isn't done, frog legs will be worth more than gold. I like fried frog legs more than chicken wings," Ben said.

"Ben, really? That's the kind of attitude you take about an entire class of creatures? Don't you realize the balance of nature is sensitive?" Matt had his hands firmly placed on hips, speaking like it was first hour biology 101.

Ben rolled his eyes. "Yeah, I know. I was making a joke. Sounds to me like you've had your nose to the grindstone for too long. You need to lighten up a bit. If I had a Snickers bar, I'd give it to you."

"Hah! I love those commercials. Yeah, who do you think he'd turn into?" Logan chimed.

"Hmmm," Ben pondered. "Steve Irwin."

Matt raised his finger in protest, but Logan's hysterical laughter forced a pause.

"Crikey, mate. I think you've nailed it," Logan said in his best Aussie accent.

A discomfited smirk widened across Matt's mouth. "Okay, okay, I get it. I have been wound a little tight lately."

"Just lately?" Ben said.

"Don't pile on. My life's been hectic these past several months. I was keeping my head barely above water, and now that we're leaving on the three week excursion, I'm not sure how I'm going to keep my research schedule." Matt rubbed the back of his neck.

"Don't worry, Matt. Either we'll discover something really important in Patagonia, or we'll come back empty handed. Previous plans won't matter if we discover new species. But if we find nothing, I'll help you catch up anyway I can," Logan said.

"I appreciate that. We'll just cross that bridge when we come to it." Matt grabbed another sack, and the other two followed his lead.

Natasha had just removed her purse from the locker in the break room when Alex Klasse walked in. She looked up at him, her eyes wide with vibrant youth. Something else was there, something he hoped would last forever. A longing; a sadness; a wanting.

"Leaving early?" he asked.

"Yeah. The guys said they'd take care of the last pallet. I wanted to do some shopping."

"I'm really looking forward to the trip. Hopefully, we'll be able to sally forth on our own and do some *research*." His eyebrows raised in anticipation.

"Are you crazy? Your wife is coming with us. I'm going to pretend you have the plague and avoid you *and her* as much as possible." Natasha had lowered her voice into a whisper, looking past Alex's shoulder through the doorway.

Alex wanted to take her in his arms and kiss the full lips on her radiant, mocha brown face. Natasha had resurrected the young man he once was from layers of life's trials and scars. The greatest poison, he came to realize, was Susan, his wife of twenty years.

"I was shocked when Susan said she wanted to come. She's never asked to go with me on my other finds. Of course, she has little tolerance for Cryptozoology—throwing it in with UFOs and ghost stories. At first she placated me—went along with my *hobby*, but as the years went on, she became more and more bitter about it. Saying the time I wasted on following up on sightings would be better spent on time spent with her. At first, I did see her point, but didn't want to give up something that has fascinated me all my life. Susan's not one to compromise. So the distance between us has only grown since then."

"So get a divorce."

Natasha had finally said the D word. She had drawn a line in the sand. Alex had wondered how deep they would go in the relationship before she hinted at ultimatums.

"It's not that simple," Alex said, rubbing his bottom teeth on his upper lip.

"I know divorce isn't simple. But it can take a long time. So after the trip, get it started. The sooner it starts, the sooner it ends."

"Natasha...I..." Alex heaved out a breath of air. "A few years back I skimmed some money from one of my university grants and used the funds for a Bigfoot trip in northern California. I actually got away with it, but Susan found out. We had a big fight over it—me risking our livelihood over some, 'stupid bullshit,' as she called it. I threatened divorce then. She made it clear that if I divorced her she'd expose the theft. We eventually made up and continued our benign relationship. She had me then, and still has me where she wants me. The only way I can divorce her is for it to be her idea. She needs to want to leave me. I've been hoping she'd meet someone else and have an affair. I've even thought of sending her an anonymous free membership to Ashley Madison."

"Ashley Madison, what's that?"

"It's a website where married people join to find others to have affairs with. It's like Match dot com or other dating sites."

"Why'd they name it Ashley Madison? That's a strange name for a dating service."

"I don't know. But I guess *Fuck dot com* was a little too *in your face*." Alex grinned, and then felt Natasha's finger poke him in the ribs.

She giggled.

Natasha got his humor—that was one reason why he was so enamored with her. And she had said his humor was one reason she was so enamored with him.

The East Indian beauty leaned toward him as if she were hungry for a kiss.

"I thought you went shopping?" Matt's voice called from the doorway.

Alex's heart plunged to his stomach. He was mere seconds from getting busted red-handed. That wouldn't be good at any time, but had that happened now before the trip—total disaster. From now on he had to do a better job at keeping his guard up, at least until he found a way to get Susan out of his life.

Natasha coolly tilted her head around Alex, who then moved out of the way and to her side. "I'm leaving now. I had a couple of things to discuss with the professor." She stepped toward the doorway and passed Matt, with Ben and Logan behind him. "See you guys later," she said, not looking back.

Alex saw Matt turn his head and give him a discerning gaze. How long had he been there at the doorway? Did Matt hear anything? He didn't think so. When Natasha lowered her voice, Alex had lowered his. Still, if Matt heard them whispering that would raise some suspicion. But for now there was no use in worrying about the unknown.

"I guess it's time for me to shove off too. When we get the call, I'll meet you guys at the airport." Alex removed his hardhat, placed it on a shelf next to others, and used his fingers to comb his hair over to the side.

He strode out of the break room doorway past Matt, Ben, and Logan, shoving off with a wink and a nod.

CHAPTER 5

The whine of the Chinook's Honeywell twin turboshaft engines mixed with the tandem rotors 60-foot blades chopping the air. The headphones Natasha wore reduced the noise inside the cabin to a warm hum. Curious, she slightly pulled one side of the headphones away from her ear. The roar thumped her hard, shocking her a bit. She quickly secured the headphone back in place.

Two hours had passed from the time Ace Corporation's private jet touched down at a remote airport in Chile. The flight left at 10 p.m. from Miami and had taken close to twelve hours to get there. Once the plane rolled to a stop, she and the others stepped off the plane onto rollup stairs, and then climbed aboard the massive helicopter waiting to bring them to their final destination. It took less than a half hour from touchdown for the airport employees to unload and ferry their gear to the Chinook. Once everything had been secured, the three-man crew fired up the engines and flew the aircraft into the sky.

The time zone had shifted by two hours. Everyone advanced their watches. The satellite phones issued by Ace Corporation automatically updated.

Natasha brought the back of her hand up to her mouth and hid a yawn. Jetlag had been weighing on her before arriving in Chile. She managed to catch a few hours of sleep, but that only happened after cutting up with the others on the jet. Everyone was wired to the max—excited to finally be on the way. Well, not everyone. Susan Klasse had separated herself early on during the festivities, choosing a seat near the back of the jet, and spending quality time with a thick paperback.

The group had been told to eat a good meal before departing. But to everyone's delight, Ace Corporation had stocked the jet with a variety of meats and cheeses, as well as bread, crackers, fruit, and pastries. No rubber chicken and plastic peas for this in-flight meal. To top that, the refrigerator was stocked with various brands of beer and an assortment of wine, as well as bottled water and soft drinks.

At first, Professor Klasse forbade anyone from drinking alcohol. Shocked expressions and silence immediately followed his declaration. Ben being Ben, and thank goodness for it, had no problem challenging Alex for making such a pointless demand. Ben stiffened to attention, and said, "Yes sir, oh great and wise B'wana."

Alex turned a bit red while the others laughed. He cast his gaze to the floor, and after a few moments, lifted it back up and shrugged his shoulders. All he said was, *Sorry*, and the party began. Apparently, Alex had realized he overreacted. Either that, or he had spied the opened bottles of Guinness Ben held in his hands. Every man has a weakness. Alex Klasse never met an open bottle of Guinness he didn't drink.

The Chinook's cabin wasn't nearly as comfortable as the jet's. The seat's cushion had little spring left; its construction engineered with strength and weight in mind. The back of the seat irritated her left shoulder blade. Natasha estimated up to 50 people could cramp onboard. There were only six members of their group, and everyone except Alex and Susan had marked off a good piece of personal space.

At one-point Matt left his seat and stepped over by Natasha, who sat by one of the four windows. She thought that a bit strange, as Matt could have chosen more than one window to look out of with no one sitting around. He didn't linger for long, and for a moment acted like he was going to sit next to her. Instead, he meandered over to the other side of the cabin and sat by a vacant window. Not long after, his eyes closed, and his head leaned over—fast asleep.

Alex sat next to Susan, across from Natasha. On more than one occasion Natasha looked over to see Susan gazing her way—and not turning away when she saw Natasha staring back. This brought some unsettling feelings, and Natasha feared she would show her nervousness and raise unwanted suspicion. Alex had his eyes closed. He didn't look like he was asleep or even resting, for that matter. Natasha could tell he was in deep thought. She so wished she could read his mind right now. After she had suggested he divorce Susan, the few times they spoke before the trip, she hadn't mentioned it again. Alex certainly didn't bring it up, perhaps feeling the story of the embezzlement becoming exposed as the end all. Well, it wasn't the end all. She didn't want to share Alex with Susan. If Alex didn't make a move and find a way out of the marriage, then Natasha would have to woman-up and break away.

That thought left her cold and empty. Her eyes moistened, and her nostrils burned a bit. She turned her attention toward Ben.

Even though he didn't look comfortable, Ben worked on book of crossword puzzles while stretched out across the seat—his back on the seat cushion—and the book upside down. He'd hold the book with one hand while he scribbled in the answers with the other, a gravitational challenge that seemed more trouble than what it was worth.

Logan had been hacking away at the keyboard on his satellite phone. Natasha used to think he had spent an extraordinary amount of time text messaging to his friends. Later she found out he kept a personal journal and made entries throughout the day. Logan had told her he had started a journal while in puberty, around twelve years old. As hormones kicked in, many kids found their world turned upside down. For Logan, walling himself from others was the safest refuge. But the walls keeping others out became a prison for him, slowly killing his very soul as each day passed. Feeling like there was no one to talk to, especially anyone in his family, Logan checked out a few self-help books from the library. Advice ranged from pertinent to absurd. The one thing that ultimately worked for him was starting a journal. Writing the words to paper acted as a confession. Even though no one else saw it, his thoughts were no longer caged inside. With each passing day more layers of hurt peeled away from his wounds, finally settling the conflict of who he was, and what he wanted from life. No one had a right to judge him for who he loved or why he did so. By the age of 16, he spoke his mind willingly and freely to everyone—consequences be damned. Of course, there had been conflicts. But with each hurtful pruning, his resolve only grew stronger. His *affliction* had become his strength, and there was no obstacle in life that he wouldn't find his way around.

Natasha removed the satellite phone from her jacket and opened her contact list. After several keystrokes and pushing send, she sent Logan a message:

We should be there soon. You excited?

Logan continued to type, even though he briefly gazed Natasha's way; apparently he wanted to finish logging his thoughts.

I feel like crap. I need some caffeine.

After a long minute, Logan stopped typing and closed his eyes, leaned his head back, and flexed his neck. He looked over at Natasha and started typing again.

I miss the open bar on the jet.

Natasha smiled as she read the message and wished she would have passed on the last glass of wine. Logan held his own when it came to drinking alcohol. He was a fun drunk, and she had never seen him hung over—even after a long night of partying. Logan claimed that dancing was alcohol's equalizer, ridding it quickly from the body.

Logan sent another text.

How weird is it?

Natasha read the message and gazed back at Logan.

Logan tilted his head toward Susan Klasse.

Natasha typed:

A little worse than I imagined. I'm managing.

A reply followed:

I warned you this day would come.

Yes, Logan had warned her that nothing good could come out of her secret affair with Alex. Natasha chewed on her lower lip and looked at Logan, a displeased expression on her face sent the message she didn't want to be preached to again. Logan was the only one who knew about the illicit relationship. Natasha had prided herself on how well she hid her attraction for Alex from others. But with Logan, he suspected something early on and mentioned it. Of course, she had denied it, calling a desire for the older man *crazy*. Natasha was crazy, *crazy* in love. When she opened up to Logan, because he kept pushing the accusation, he said her feelings were just an infatuation, and that they would pass even before the semester was over. As intuitive as Logan was, he got that part wrong. Her love for Alex was so strong she was almost to the point of abandoning her studies and running away with him to where ever they could find happiness.

"Attention. We will begin our descent in a moment and touchdown at thirteen thirty," a crewmember's voice said over the intercom.

Everyone stirred. Ben quickly moved to a sitting position and abandoned his crossword puzzle. Natasha tightened her seat belt—she had loosened it during the flight.

Matt looked up at Natasha, and while smiling, lifted a thumb-up. If he noticed Logan staring intently at him, he didn't show it.

The sour expression worn on Susan's face didn't dissipate. Alex grabbed the bottom of his shirt and pulled it taut while sitting higher in his seat.

The Chinook dove through the air faster than Natasha's stomach could handle. She felt a bit of nausea and reached for the barf bag under her seat. It was there, but the sick feeling passed before she pulled it out.

Natasha wasn't sure how high they were to begin with. Helicopters can't go above 10,000 feet without supplied air. She didn't think they were near that high during the trip. The descent slowed as she watched out the window. The vast forest thinned as it neared the towering mountain range. A small settlement of tents and a strange looking vehicle marked the landing site.

The ground neared, debris flew into the air, and the mighty bird set down on *terra firma*.

CHAPTER 6

Alex saw the blades' shadows slow to a stop as he watched through the Chinook's window. He turned his gaze toward the mountains and followed the rugged area up to where the snow and ice formed, unable from his vantage point to see the peaks.

Ace Corporation had been brief with details, telling Alex that information was *sensitive* and demanded secrecy, but that all would be revealed upon their arrival in Northern Patagonia. There were times he felt stupid for not pushing the issue—when he fretted over the safety of his group. But the corporation's representative had been so professional, so smooth, practically convincing Alex that details would do nothing but distract him from his revolutionary work. Of course, Alex felt that if he put up too much of a ruckus, Ace Corporation would find another team to go in.

He and the rest of his team, including Susan, had to sign confidentiality contracts. Even the University didn't know the real reason they were going to South America. Ace Corporation offered the grant to study cryptid reports in Brazil. With Alex's reputation, nothing seemed out of the ordinary, and the mission was approved by the University's board of supervisors.

Despite all the undercover antics, the contracts plainly stated that Alex and every member of his group would share in the credit if dinosaurs were found to inhabit the area. The deal as a whole was favorable, and Alex signed the dotted line. The fantasy now had become reality. It was time to set foot on new land.

Ben was the first to remove his headphones—tossing them on the seat next to his backpack, which he then hung from one shoulder. First in line, as usual.

Natasha fumbled with her seat belt before it snapped open. Even though the hours of fatigue weighed on her face, she was still radiantly beautiful.

He caught Susan shooting jealousy daggers a time or two at Natasha. Which wasn't an unusual reaction for Susan to have toward any women in Alex's vicinity. She might not have much desire left for him, but she certainly didn't want any other woman to spark an interest in her man.

Susan knew one of his female students was coming on the trip, but he doubted that was the only reason she demanded to accompany him. If there was fame and fortune to be had, she wanted in on it. And if fame and fortune did come, Alex so hoped Susan would rid herself of him. That would be a greater gift than saddling up a T-rex and riding it cross-country.

Logan had his backpack over both shoulders and helped Matt as he struggled to get his left arm past the strap. Once on, Logan zipped an open pocket and adjusted the length of the straps so the backpack hung evenly.

The rear door slowly moved, creating an opening nearly as large as the cabin. Alex imagined from the outside the Chinook looked like some giant fish with its mouth gaping open. The air wafting inside was slightly warmer than it had been in the cabin. It brought with it a slight sulfur odor, and then he remembered the active volcano on the other side of the mountains.

A one-man greeting reception walked from the side into view as Ben stepped off the loading ramp onto the ground. The man looked to be a little older than Alex, perhaps in his sixties, and wore jungle camo fatigues. His gray beard was short and neatly trimmed.

Ben waited for the others to line up beside him, each looking toward the man for instruction. The man, though, kept his gaze toward Alex. It was obvious he wanted to speak to the person in charge.

Alex matched gazes with the man, and as he neared, he read 'Cooper' embroidered on the man's light jacket.

"Where are the others? I thought there would be more sent here to protect us. I don't have a good feeling about this," Susan turned and whispered.

When did Susan *ever* have a good feeling about anything new? "I'm sure there're more inside the tents. Stop worrying, and let me handle this." Alex moved from behind his wife, and stepped over to the side of the ramp in front of Cooper. The ramp had him elevated a couple of feet from Cooper's eye level.

"Hello. I'm Alex Klasse," Alex said matter of factly. He kept his thumbs inside the backpack's straps, making no attempt to shake hands. Life had taught him on first introductions to greet others in the like manner they greeted him. The procedure generally earned him instant respect.

"Pleased to meet you, Mr. Klasse. My name is Vincent Cooper. I'll be heading the expedition for the Ace Corporation." Dark glasses hid Cooper's eyes. Though his voice had a pleasant tone, his stiff expression marred his cordial greeting. "I'm sure you and your crew must be tired. Please follow me for some refreshments and to meet the rest of the group." Cooper waited for Susan and Alex to step off the ramp before turning and heading toward the encampment.

"We're in the Army now. We're in the Army now. You'll never get rich, you son-of-a-bitch, we're in the Army now," Ben sang in a low voice as he marched.

"Ben, mind your manners," Alex said.

"Yes, B'wana." Ben returned to his normal assertive gait.

Alex held his tongue, mostly because the others seemed to be slightly embarrassed by Ben's outbreak. Ben was just being Ben. An excuse they used for him all the time—maybe enabling him more than they should.

Cooper waited in front of one of the larger tents and pointed with his left hand. "Please step inside. Watch the entrance, the canvas is bunched up, and you might trip."

Ben pulled a flap to the side and stepped through. Matt followed, and then Logan and Natasha.

Before Susan entered, Cooper said, "Mr. Klasse, I need you to join me in the next tent—to discuss things."

"Alex, I—"

"No need to worry, Mrs. Klasse. I won't keep him very long. Go on inside and get comfortable," Cooper said.

"Join the others, Susan. The man says we won't be long." Alex had let Cooper know that he was willing to trust him at his word. Now, it would be up to Cooper to prove himself.

Susan held her gaze on Alex long enough to realize he wasn't going to change his mind, scowled, and abruptly stepped inside.

Cooper had headed for a smaller tent a few yards away. Alex followed him until they were both inside.

A thin plastic table a few feet wide and a couple of feet deep set between two foldout chairs opposite of each other.

"Please, have a seat," Cooper said.

The backpack slid off Alex's shoulders. He placed it next to the chair and sat, wary of his seat's sturdiness.

Cooper walked over to an open box next to other boxes and gear. He took out a clear bottle containing light amber liquid and two glass tumblers. It was obviously alcohol of some sort, but with no label on the bottle it was impossible to identify. He then opened the bottle and poured equal portions into each glass.

Cooper took his seat and raised his glass.

Alex lifted his glass, and the two made a silent toast.

Smooth, rich smokiness caressed his palate, and the gentle fire of spirits warmed his throat. "That was delightful. Judging from the bottle, I was expecting homemade 'shine, and it tasting like lighter fluid. That was a single malt Scotch, one that I've not had the pleasure to drink before."

"I'm personal friends with my employer. This Scotch is from a private distillery and not available to the public. Drinking Scotch, 'is a toast to civilization, a tribute to the continuity of culture, a manifesto of man's determination to use the resources of nature to refresh mind and body and enjoy to the full the senses with which he has been endowed.' " Cooper set the glass down and put his hands on the table.

"David Daiches."

"Yes. I memorized that quote the first time I read it. It seems we at least have one thing in common, Mr. Klasse. But you should know I read your file, and I do know you appreciate a good Scotch whiskey."

"You have the advantage then. Details of who would accompany us in country were mostly left to my imagination. And I have a *very* wild imagination."

Cooper chuckled. "Yes, your file mentioned that too. I wanted this one-on-one meeting so that we could be better acquainted. Less distractions. Now, I try to run a tight ship, but I'm not a micro manager. As a representative of Ace Corporation, I have goals and objectives different from yours. However, the soldiers under my keep are here to protect both of our interests. You will pursue the hunt for extinct forms of life, and I will pursue my interest."

"Which is…"

"Commodities, Mr. Klasse. I'm sure you at least tried to look up Ace Corporation on the internet to see who wanted to fund this trip."

"Yes, I did. Ace Corp is a financial institution that deals in commodities. I never made a connection as to why they wanted to sponsor a trip to find dinosaurs."

"Well, that's where I come in. I'm a geologist. Got my degree after a few stints in Vietnam. I'm here to scope out the area and return with a report of the natural resources I find. There was no way the local government here would allow our excursion if they knew the full truth. That's why we wanted to use the story of *finding cryptid life in an uncharted area* as a façade to hide behind. The story has even more credibility because the trip was arranged by Southwood University and has Professors and students involved. The heavy equipment we brought in with us was done through a series of bribes and covert missions. To lay the cards on the table, we are using you as a front for our own greedy purpose. That's why the contracts stipulate that any extinct animals found in the region can't be revealed for three years. Those three years will be used by the Ace Corporation to gain control of the interest in the region and all the spoils it contains."

Alex maintained his poker face. Nothing Cooper said had surprised him, in fact, he felt stupid for not figuring out the plot on his own. So, he was being used by an evil corporation to plunder a pristine area of the world. Nothing honorable about that. One thing for certain, you can't eat honor, and after all his failures in *chasing Bigfoot*, instead of being known as a *kook* by many of his peers, he had a chance to become respected—in everyone's eyes. Besides, they had all come this far, and if he didn't do it, someone else would. "Capitalism at its finest. Mr. Cooper—"

"Coop."

"Okay, Coop, call me Alex. I appreciate the directness and look forward to working with you to achieve both of our goals."

"Wonderful, this proves we have more in common." Cooper picked up the bottle of Scotch and poured a serving in each glass. "The area we're about to explore essentially has been walled off from mankind since way before our ancestors left the trees and walked on two legs. There is an active volcano in the expanse, but it shouldn't present any problems. One theory is the mountains, combined with the poisonous gases released by the volcano, acted as a deterrent for curious explorers. Recent earthquakes have opened a few pathways in the mountain ranges that allow us easier access. The mountain winds make flight of any type of aircraft into the area too treacherous to attempt. That's why we have to go across ground and not just helicopter in."

"But I was told a drone took the pictures of the pterosaur," Alex said.

"Yes, and we'll have a drone with us on our trip. The pictures were taken by a drone that took a flight through one of the new openings, and it flew lower than the wind turbulence. We had a two-man expedition go in hundreds of miles south of here. That passageway is too narrow for the vehicle we'll be riding in. What interested Ace Corporation in this area was recent data from a new satellite set in orbit by a private contractor. We were able to match certain signatures in this area of Patagonia with others in the world, which suggest the commodities we are interested in are available."

"What kind of commodities?" Alex asked.

Cooper smiled. "Alex, sorry, but some details must remain private." He picked up his glass of Scotch and lifted it toward Alex.

Alex pressed his lips together and raised his eyebrows. "Understood."

He lifted his glass, and the two downed another round.

***

Natasha entered the dimly lit tent and saw several men dressed in similar garb as the one who met them off the Chinook. They were a motley looking bunch, and she couldn't help but feel a measure of intimidation.

One of them stood with his hands together in front of his chest. He flexed his fingers in one hand against those of the other, as if waiting for everyone to enter before speaking. Three others sat a table. Two stared their way, and the other was in the process of cleaning a handgun. The last man, a really big guy, was by himself several feet away near the back of the tent. He sat in a chair, a notebook and pen in his hand, and after looking up at Natasha, he dropped his head and began writing.

Ben, Matt, and Logan waited stiffly to the side. She was surprised to see Ben act as if he were somewhat intimidated too.

The next person stepped into the tent, so she moved over by Logan. It was Susan Klasse. Alex didn't follow behind her. Neither did the man who greeted them. Before her imagination got the best of her, the man in front spoke.

"Hi, I'm the lead member of the security team. We are employed by a private military company called *Redwater*. I'm sure you've heard of the outfit. The U.S. government has kept us busy since the heat kicked up in the Mideast. My teammates call me *Chief*, you can call me Chief. My job, the security team's job, is to protect all the members on this deployment. We aren't here to tell you how to run your business, but if we feel a situation is too dangerous, we will step in and take control." Chief removed his cap and swiped his jet-black hair from front to back. "Despite what we may look like to a bunch of civilians, especially most of you of college age, we're not a bunch of blood thirsty hooligans. We are professionals. We expect to be treated that way, and we require respect. That said, we're going to be spending a lot of time together over the next three weeks, so we will get to know each other. Feel free to get to know us. We won't bite—unless we're forced to."

"Ah-ruff! Ah-ruff!" a slightly chubby Redwater member, looking to be in his forties, sitting at the table by Chief, barked.

Chief smiled. "That man, who could pass for Curly of the Three Stooges, is John Jones. We call him Caveman. You'll find out why when you get to know him. He likes to cut up a bit. But I warn you, don't challenge him to a wrestling match. He hasn't lost one yet."

"Hi ya'all," Caveman said, waving his hand like he was the king in a parade.

Chief continued, "Sitting closest to me is Mr. Henry Hunter, a seasoned veteran who fought in Desert Storm. We call him Suge. You don't call him Suge unless you ask him first."

The black man lifted a hand in acknowledgement. He still had some youth about him. Natasha thought him to be in his thirties and ruggedly handsome.

"Next to Suge we have Tim Colter. We call him Bats. You can call him Bats too. His drawl gives away that he's from Texas. He's recently returned from Afghanistan."

Bats was the one cleaning the handgun. He stood and slightly tipped his hat toward Natasha and the rest. The effort was a mock gesture at best. He looked like he was in his forties too.

"The big guy in the corner is Clint Perry, otherwise known as Meat—for obvious reasons. He's from Maui and quite the artist. His dream is to save up enough to open a tattoo parlor. If any of you would like a tattoo on this trip, I'm sure he'd be happy to oblige."

"All my inks are non-toxic," Meat said, holding his pen up as if ready to draw the outline.

Meat was a big man, not fat—but massive. Tall, wide, with finely chiseled features on a square head. The pen had looked more like a toothpick when he held it up in his large hand. He was definitely a native of the Hawaiian Islands. The Samoan features of his face made it look like he had a perpetual happy expression.

A dolly pushed through the tent entrance with items from the Chinook. A member of Redwater steered it to the side. A second dolly followed, pushed by another Rainwater member. The two were definitely the oldest of the security team, and surprisingly, were identical twins.

"This is Ron Bartel," Chief said, pointing.

"I'm Don," Don Bartel said.

"Yeah, that happens a lot," Chief said. "That's Ron," he correctly pointed.

"Roll Tide," Ron said, his South Alabama accent thick.

"Don't worry if you get these two confused. They answer to whatever name you call them. Ron and Don first saw action in Vietnam. Since then, they're either hunting, fishing, or fighting a war."

"Except for a few hours on Saturdays when it's football season," Don said.

Matt stepped away from the group, and said, "I'm Matt King, associate professor of Zoology at Southwood University. I think I speak for all of us in saying how excited we are to be here and pleased Ace Corporation has gone to great lengths to offer protection. We will certainly cooperate any way we can. I'm sure there's a protocol for us to learn."

"There is, and we'll teach you everything you need to know before we head out," Chief said.

Ron and Don pushed the dollies over the side of the tent next to a long table. One of the two, Natasha wasn't sure if it was Ron or Don, began lighting cans of sterno. The other unloaded large aluminum pans covered in foil onto the table.

Matt continued, "Our leader, Professor Alex Klasse, must be with the Mr. Cooper who met us off the helicopter. Let me introduce the rest of my group." Matt moved away from his crew so as not to block anyone from view. "First in line is Ben Wilson."

Ben closed his left eye, made a gesture with his right hand like it was a gun, and then flexed his thumb like he fired it in Chief's direction.

"Next is Logan Sandler."

Logan gave a firm, polite nod.

"Natasha Kamdar."

Natasha smiled and slightly cocked her head to the side, still feeling a bit awkward. She was about to spend three weeks with a group of strange men. The thought marred the excitement of dinosaur hunting.

"Ben, Logan, and Natasha are students about to enter graduate school. Lastly we have Susan Klasse, wife of professor Klasse."

"Pleased to meet you, gentlemen," Susan said.

Natasha had never heard Susan Klasse use such a pleasant tone this whole trip. Apparently the woman was capable of turning on the charm when she wanted.

"Chief, food's about ready," Don said.

"All right. Guys, this will be the best meal we'll have until we come back. So, chow down," Chief said.

"Not unless I get me a Brontosaurus. I'm gonna make burgers out of that thing," Caveman said as he rose from the table, hurrying to be first in line.

The security crew wasn't bashful and certainly didn't act like gracious hosts. It was every man for himself in the food line.

Ben spread his hands like *What the hell*, and headed for the end of the line. Logan followed, and Matt hung back, letting Susan go next, and he took his position behind Natasha.

"You okay?" Matt asked.

"Sure, why wouldn't I be?" Natasha actually appreciated his concern. Where the hell was Alex? But she didn't want to get too chummy with Matt. Nothing good could come from that.

"I didn't mean anything by it. I feel—and I can tell you and the others feel it too—that this isn't going to be a Disney adventure. It's real, and it's probably going to get rough out there. I just want you to know, I'll be watching out for you. So, if you need anything…"

Natasha almost snapped a dismissive retort, but hesitated, not wanting to come across negatively. "Thanks." *There, just leave it at that.*

The big guy sitting alone at a table, Meat, was the only member of his team not in line. He remained in his chair, vigorously dotting a page on his notebook with the pen.

Meat sat near the end of the line, and as Natasha approached, she saw what he'd been working on. It was a black and white drawing of her head and face. A red rose adorned her hair on one side. The large man looked up and caught her gaze.

"Do you like it?" He stopped drawing and turned the picture for proper view.

"That's amazing. I can't believe you drew that in the short amount of time we've been here." The picture had a photographic quality to it. A technique she'd seen somewhere before.

"Ah, it's nothing. Beauty always inspires me. I draw a lot of flowers because of that. That's why I put a rose in your hair. Beauty compliments beauty," Meat said without any lecherous intent in his tone.

Matt started to say something, but Natasha raised her hand to wave him off, and said, "Thank you. That's nice of you to say."

"You're welcome." Meat tore the page from the notebook and offered it to her. "Here, have a Clint Perry original. Hopefully one day it'll be worth a million dollars." The big guy laughed and shook his head as if boyishly embarrassed at the suggestion.

Natasha took the picture and held it closer, drinking in the details. She remembered the technique used to draw her face was called stippling. A pen is used to make dots, and the denser the collection of dots, the darker the picture. That's why Meat's drawing resembled a black and white photograph. The rose was just drawn and looked a bit cartoonish.

Meat got up from his chair and filed in line behind Matt. Some had already sat down to eat.

Natasha wasn't sure what was on the menu, but roasted meat of some sort mixed with stale air in the tent, making her aware she was hungry. "I hope there's bacon. I can never get enough bacon."

"Well, it looks like the party has started without me," Alex said. He stood near the tent's entrance, with Cooper next to him.

CHAPTER 7

Natasha stretched her arms high and yawned. It was shortly after they ate, around 3 o'clock in the afternoon. The air carried a slight irritant, and the sun was well into its daily journey across the sky. Breathtaking mountains to the west formed a wall as far as the eye could see. Beyond that ancient barrier the adventure began. At this point, it called like a Siren to a lonely sailor lost at sea. The anticipation of discovering what was on the other side had her mind wandering.

Lunch was better than she had expected. The food loaded on the Chinook had been freshly prepared and had remained warm on the ride over. She was told MREs would sustain them for the three-week trip. Even though entrees like Meatballs with Marinara Sauce, Mexican Style Chicken Stew, and Lemon Pepper Tuna sounded delicious, Natasha doubted the dishes would taste as good as those with the same name at a nice restaurant.

Chief and a few of his men had gathered her crew behind the tents by the strange vehicle she first saw when they landed in the Chinook. The vehicle was longer than a bus and about as tall. It was unique to anything she had ever seen, although, according to Chief, the All-Terrain Tracked Carrier had been used in various configurations by many nations of the world since early 2000. Its primary function was to act as a troop carrier.

The ATTC, or Warthog as this variant was named, looked like a stretched Humvee with tracks—like a tank—instead of wheels. The vehicle was large enough to easily hold the 14-member gang heading into the great unknown. Attached behind the main vehicle, called the rear cabin, a similarly configured troop carrier—minus the cab—doubled troop capacity. For this trip, that's where all the supplies were stored. And to one-up that, a car sized smaller version of the Warthog rested on a platform behind the rear cabin. Up front, the smaller vehicle had a blade similar to that of a bulldozer and a machine gun mounted on the roof.

In a way, the Warthog looked like a military version of an RV, all the comforts of home as you cruised to your destination, and a smaller vehicle to detach and take quick trips away from the monstrous home base.

"This baby may look big and bulky and a pain in the ass to drive, but it isn't. It has hydraulic steering for ease of maneuverability and rubber tracks to soften the ride. It has a very light footprint, and can travel through water, mud, sand, swamp, and snow. It's tall enough inside to stand and move around in, so your ass doesn't fall asleep. It's even air-conditioned," Chief said, slowly pacing from one side to the other in front of the group. He'd maintained eye contact with someone at all times.

"What kind of sound system does it have?" Ben asked.

Chief stopped cold in his tracks, and shifted a lazy eyed gaze at the athletic student. "It's called, *Shut the fuck up when I'm giving instruction.*"

Alex looked over at Ben and slightly shook his head.

Ben raised animated eyebrows and nodded. "I like it."

Chief ignored the comment and pointed to the roof of the cab in the front. "Now, the gun you see on the roof jutting from behind the armored plate, is a weapon specially designed for Ace Corporation. In fact, all of the weapons on this trip are custom made. Only the Redwater troops will have the custom weapons, because of their specialized nature. You, however, will be issued standard semi-automatic pistols for personal protection. That is, only if you know how to use one. We don't have much time before we head out, but Ron and Don will give you a quick lesson when issuing your guns later on." Chief raised his arm and motioned to someone behind the group.

Ron—or Don—stepped over with an assault-type looking gun. Natasha had heard of AR-15s and AK-47s, but didn't really know how to differentiate the two.

Chief took the rifle and held it in front of him. "This is called the JNY-Seven. We just call it a *Seven*. This rifle holds one hundred rounds of custom ammunition. The bullets are caseless, so we won't be dropping brass all over the countryside. The projectile may be small, but it packs a nice sized wallop. There is a stable compound in the bullet that reacts upon impact. In other words, it's an exploding bullet. We're not entirely sure what we'll be facing out there, but we will be prepared." He pulled the rifle closer and held it in one arm, using the other hand to point. "This on top is a grenade launcher, used for widespread damage in a chosen area. There are three grenades in reserve. On the side here, is a version of a rocket-propelled grenade—for distance. The rifle will shoot single shots, three round bursts, or fully automatic. The trigger mechanism is actually part of a separate piece by itself, a pistol." Chief pushed in a button, the hand-grip-trigger mechanism and a short section of gun barrel detached as a single piece—a handgun. "The rifle still can be used to fire grenades. This pistol is exactly like the sidearms the Redwater's carry, and is interchangeable with the one in the rifle. Helps in battlefield situations. The pistol by itself can hold up to thirty rounds of ammo. So, I've run my yap enough for now. Any questions?" Chief looked directly at Ben.

"So where's the gas stations to fuel this thing up? I know oil comes from dead dinosaurs, but I don't think we'll have enough time to make our own," Ben said, a serious expression on his face. Apparently, he was determined to make a valid point without compromising his sarcastic nature.

Chief quickly pointed a finger at Ben. "Good question. We won't need to fuel up during the trip."

Logan raised his hand. "Does it run on a fuel cell? Is it solar powered in some way? I don't see any solar panels."

"We got something better than that. It's nuclear powered," Chief said.

"Nuclear power? Are you serious?" Alex sounded truly amazed.

"Yes. Not only the Warthog, but also the four-man vehicle on the rear. We call that the *Mule*. It's nuclear powered too. We could run either vehicle three months without stopping before we'd have to change the rods."

"But this thing is huge. Even if we make it past the mountains, there aren't any roads for us to travel on. And from what we're told, there's thick forest covering some large areas. Are we just going to drive around aimlessly? What if on day one we find that we can't go in any direction?" Susan said, standing slightly in front of Alex, her left hand on her hip.

Natasha saw Chief's expression soften as the woman spoke. A warm smile spread across his lips. So, Mr. Chief had taken a liking to the witch. Natasha could see why; Chief hadn't spent any time with the sourpuss. Susan was an attractive woman, though. She kept her body in shape and only needed a little lipstick and eye makeup to pretty up her face. Natasha was seeing this now as if for the first time. Jealousy had blinded her from the beginning. This made her even bitterer toward Alex. Maybe he had other reasons—emotional reasons—not blackmail—as to why he didn't divorce her.

"We aren't going in as blind as you think. Even though the entire area is hidden under clouds thanks to magma being so close to the surface and the cold air blowing above the mountains, we still were able to make a map. Satellites using special radar mapped the surface down to one meter in length. So, with our onboard GPS, we have a map that shows us where we can travel. It also shows other points of interest like the location of the volcano, the various lakes, and even a nice size river. We might not be able to take the most direct route, but we shouldn't have a problem getting to any point we want," Chief said.

"Yeah, but this thing looks slow. How far can we explore in a three week period?" Logan asked.

"On the open road, a Warthog can go up to forty miles an hour. This version can top sixty. But, because there aren't any roads in Patagonia, as the lady pointed out, we'll just make the best time we can." Chief paused, and motioned with his fingers, asking for more questions.

"Let's talk about the gun on the roof," Alex said, and stole a quick glance toward Natasha.

She saw a strange reaction on Alex's face. *What's up with him?* Then it dawned on her. Alex first looked at her, and then looked at Matt standing next to her. Alex wasn't happy about something, and she thought she knew what that something was. It was the way Matt was looking at her and the story his body language told. Alex was jealous, and Natasha loved it.

Alex focused his attention back on Chief. "That looks like a deadly weapon. I'm sure it's necessary for our protection, but I hope this would be used as a last resort. I'd rather run from a unique life form than fight it to the death. How sad would it be to come across an animal long thought extinct only to kill it? I'd rather not make the journey at all if I knew that would be the outcome."

Natasha thought worrying about that now was too little too late. But perhaps Alex was trying to tell Chief in a non-threatening way not to shoot first and ask questions later.

"Professionals don't kill for pleasure, Mr. Klasse. And as professionals our job is to achieve the mission's various goals. The most important goal is the safety of everyone. At any cost. That said, we do have different types of ammunition we can load into the gun. When have some non-lethal ammo—you might call them rubber bullets—as well as the deadlier type. We even have some tranquilizer rounds, just in case we want to take one down to study," Chief said.

"That's good to hear. We have options. And I hope you'll include me in any decision where force will be used against the indigenous life," Alex said.

"Not a problem, Mr. Klasse," Chief said in a conciliatory tone. "*If* time allows, of course."

Power negotiations were on going. Natasha doubted they wouldn't stop until the mission was complete and they were back on the Chinook heading home.

"Any more questions before we issue your weapons?" Chief waited and watched heads shake back at him. "Good. Ron, take 'em to the rear cabin, and fix them up."

Ron stepped up and took Chief's place as he walked away. "You heard the man, step this way. Roll Tide." The man spoke the cheer *Roll Tide* slowly, as if the words were delicious and needed to be savored.

*

The group arrived at the Warthog's rear cabin, where Don had already matched six handguns with holsters. He was in the process of pulling ammo magazines from a bag.

"Everybody grab a gun. We're gonna have us some fun, fun, fun," Don sang to a tune one might hear at a hoedown. "The holster has a clip. Just slide that bad boy over your belt or the waist of your pants."

Ben picked up his gun and pulled it from the holster. He held the side of the gun up to his eyes. "It's not very big…Springfield Armory XD two…forty-five ACP."

"The smaller the better. Won't get in the way. Fits a woman's hands pretty good, too," Don said, and then handed two magazines to Ben. "Extended mag holds thirteen."

"Don't you have guns made for men?" Ben asked.

"Why we sure do, little buddy," Don said, a big grin crossed his face. His teeth were the lovely shade of tobacco brown. He placed his big paw on Ben's shoulder. "Those guns are for the Redwater team only."

Ron heaved out a laugh. "Good one, Don."

"He's a little green, but we'll get him nice and educated before this trip's over," Don said.

"Roll Tide," Ron said.

Ben didn't look the happiest. Alex knew Ben wasn't the one used to being teased. The young man kept his mouth shut, though. Don and Ron made a formidable tag team. Ben was definitely outmatched.

Don handed out the remainder of ammo magazines, while Ron walked over to an improvised shooting range a few yards away. Several plastic bottles had been set some fifteen or twenty feet from where Ron waited.

The way Matt clung to Natasha's side didn't set well with Alex one bit. Having Susan on the trip was like having a ball and chain around his ankle, keeping him from doing what he wanted. Worse, her presence made it as if he had the plague, keeping others from interacting with him. He had a wonderful relationship with his students back in Sarasota. He could sit with them at a pub, joke around, and still remain the authoritative figure who earned respect. Of course, he was careful not to cross certain lines to keep that order. And, of course, had failed miserably with Natasha—crossing the widest line of all. Now, Logan, Matt, Ben, and even Natasha basically treated him and Susan like they were the parents, worthy only to be ignored.

Alex was the last to receive his ammo magazines and followed the others over by Ron.

The older man waited for his captive audience and held up his handgun. "Put your mags in your pocket and look at your gun. I'm gonna learn you something. Firstly, this gun is made from polymer. Only the barrel is steel. We picked the Springfield Armory pistol mostly because of its safety features." Ron pointed to the top of the slide. "See this right here? It's the chamber indicator. When it's up, like on mine, that means there's a bullet in the chamber. Yours is down. Everybody see that?" He paused, and then moved on, turning the back of the gun toward them. "This little hole with the pin sticking out tells you if the gun is cocked— the hammer's inside the gun so you can't see it. When the pin is out like this, always treat your gun as if it's loaded. There are two more safety features. One in the trigger…see this little thing poking out from the middle?" Ron fingered the lever. "The gun can't fire unless that's pushed in. You could grab hold of the barrel and pound a nail with the grip and it won't shoot. But see this right here on the grip?" He pointed to a slim lever on the grip and pushed it in and out with his finger. "That's the grip safety. The gun won't fire unless that's pushed in, even if you pull the trigger. Everybody got that so far?"

Alex watched his wide-eyed crew. He and Susan had handled guns before and even had spent some time target shooting in their younger days. Matt had said he hunted as a boy. Logan had said he learned how to shoot while in the Boy Scouts, not by a Scout Master, but by one of the parents on unofficial outings. Ben and Natasha both had said they had not handled a handgun.

Ron continued, "Go ahead and put in a mag."

Hands went into pockets, and the bright clang of parts sliding together and snapping into place indicated the guns were loaded.

"Hold this part right here—the slide—and give it a quick pull backward." A bullet ejected from Ron's gun as another from the magazine replaced it in the chamber.

Alex snapped his back first. Susan, Ben, and Logan followed next at about the same time.

Matt watched Natasha struggle. She held the slide with her thumb and forefinger, trying to pull it back.

"No, hold the slide like this," Matt said. He grabbed his left hand on top of the slide and racked in a bullet. "Here, let me do that for you."

"Hold on there, partner. Let the little lady give it a try. It's all part of learning," Ron said.

Natasha hesitated a bit, grabbed firmly on the slide, and jacked a bullet in. "I did it!"

"Y'all can practice later. We ain't gonna get into how to break the gun down to clean it. Y'all shouldn't be shooting this thing much this trip." Ron walked over near Alex's side, no longer in front of the plastic bottles. "Point your gun at a bottle. Try to match the front sight between that grove in the rear sight, and squeeze—don't pull—squeeze the trigger slowly. This ain't no race."

Alex hit his target. Susan missed. Logan nailed his. Ben hit the ground just in front of the bottle, and it bounced up and took the bottle down.

Alex saw Matt watch for Natasha to shoot before he did. She hit Matt's target. Matt moved his aim over to her bottle. The bullet struck the ground just beyond—missing the bottle.

"Y'all got the basic handle on this?" Ron asked. "I've got other shit to do."

"If anyone needs help, I can take care of it. Thanks for the weapons and the instruction. We can manage on our own for now," Alex said.

"I left more ammo back at the rear cabin. You can shoot all you want. Just make sure to load up the mags before you turn in. I'm packing everything up tonight for the trip tomorrow," Don said.

"Will do. Thanks again—to the both of you," Alex said.

"Okay," Don said. "You ready, Ron?"

"Roll tide."

"Roll tide," Don returned. The two stepped away.

Ben turned his attention back to the target and shot two rounds; the 2nd shot hit the bottle. It was already on its side and spun off to the left.

Logan cast a curious gaze toward Matt and Natasha. Matt hovered over her like a watchful parent while she looked over at Alex.

Natasha gazed at Alex with those warm, dark eyes that could thaw an iceberg. The same eyes that melted his heart every single time she looked at him. Her parting lips reached out in a silent cry for solace. She missed him—it showed. He missed her—probably more so. There was no way he could ignore her in this moment.

"Susan, go ahead and empty the mag to get a feel for the gun. I'm going to give Natasha a hand. She looks like she's having trouble." Alex turned and walked away, not waiting for approval. If his wife had a problem with him aiding Natasha, he didn't care.

He stepped behind Natasha and turned to Matt. "Let me help her. Looks like you need the practice." Alex reached over and put his right hand on hers—the one that held the gun. He then reached over with his other hand onto her left hand, essentially embracing her from behind. Her neck smelled of gardenias and spices. It was all he could do to keep from kissing it. "Okay, what you have to do is get in a comfortable position. The fingers on your left hand should wrap around the others under the trigger. Move the gun until you sight the target and squeeze—and don't close your eyes—squeeze the trigger."

A few seconds later the gun fired. The bullet hit the target.

"I hit it!" Natasha said, showing big smile.

"All it takes is a little concentration and patience. You'll get better with practice." Alex stepped back, leaving Natasha on her own.

Matt's lips had formed a tight *O*, looking none too pleased.

Turning back toward Susan, he saw she wore the same expression as Matt.

Ben fired his gun.

Logan fired his gun.

Alex widened his stance, crossed his arms, and watched bullets fly toward the plastic bottles.

*

When Vince Cooper stepped into the tent, he saw the college crew unrolling their sleeping bags and preparing for a night's rest. He was pleased that everyone looked healthy and fit. The mission was sure to have physical challenges, and daily operations would go smoother if everyone pulled their own weight. As long as they kept out of his business, he didn't expect them to slow him down.

"Hey. I just wanted to make a quick check on you before lights out. Take care of your bedding, because you'll be bringing that with us on the trip. There aren't any spares on the Warthog. Pack it up neat and tight after you wake up. Don will be waiting at the rear cabin to load it," Coop said, his stiff demeanor had softened.

"What time do we leave? I need to set the alarm on my phone," Alex said.

"Don't bother. Ron will give you a wakeup call about an hour before sunup. We'll get dressed, eat, take care of bathroom duties, and do the final packing before we leave."

"How long do you think it will take to get past the mountains?" Logan asked. He had laid out his sleeping bag next to the side of the tent, with Matt on the other side of him, and Natasha on the other side of Matt. Ben was between Natasha and Susan, with Alex by Susan and near the other side of the tent.

"I hope it takes less than a day, but it may take longer. The roughest part of the trip is getting past the mountains. There's nothing manmade about the passage we're taking. It formed during an earthquake over a year ago. The path varies in width, and elevations shift. The computer model shows we can make it, though. But you know how real life is. The results are only as good as the guy who wrote the program," Cooper said.

"Mr. Cooper," Susan began.

"Please, Coop. You all may call me, Coop."

"Okay, I will. I was wondering if you could tell us what you personally think about this mission. Obviously, there's something of great value here or Ace Corporation wouldn't have funded us. Alex told us not to be nosy about Ace's commodities interest. But I want to know what *you* think we'll find living in Patagonia. Do you believe there are dinosaurs there?" Susan asked.

Coop raised a hand. "I'll tell you what I know. A team of two men entered Patagonia far south of here. They traveled on foot and made it about thirty miles in. During that time, when we had communication, there weren't any reports of dinosaurs of any kind. It wasn't until they were well within their journey when they first reported seeing some type of life, too far away for them to identify. Whatever it was spooked easily, and they could never get a clear view. It wasn't until their satellite phones went dead and they started the journey back that they encountered the pterosaur."

"So you *do* believe the photos were real and that extinct animals still live," Susan said.

"Yes, I do. We have more than just a few pictures. We have video of the flying reptile. It's real, and we believe there're other extinct animals alive too." Coop watched the expressions on the college crew's faces. If any of them had doubts before, they were certainly all believers now. "Our theory is, over the centuries the indigenous animals learned they were trapped by the mountains. So there was no reason for them to venture from resources—mainly water. The rivers and lakes are not located near the mountain walls. So the larger animals, like the T-rex and sauropods, if alive, won't be part of the greeting committee. We expect to meet smaller life forms first. But as we head farther in, we might find ourselves in the middle of *Jurassic Park*." Coop smiled. He had to admit such a thought made him a bit giddy too.

CHAPTER 8

Natasha bathed in a shallow stream under a narrow waterfall. She slowly wiped her cheeks and forehead with her hands, and pulled her long hair behind her back. The sound of falling water played a soothing melody, one that held Alex in its spell as he watched the new love of his life.

Warm winds carried the soft aroma of honeysuckle. He tasted it in his mouth as he breathed the sweet air. This was truly paradise. Natasha was the goddess who ruled. She was lord and master of all that was, especially him. He would worship her night and day, devoting everything toward her happiness. She had pulled him from the mire that held him captive. Alex was reborn by her touch, and needed her by his side else he wither away and die.

Natasha turned her lovely gaze his way. Her lips widened and her eyes softened as she saw him. An arm stretched out, and her hand beckoned him to join her in the river of life.

His heart swelled with immeasurable joy. He longed for her touch and sweet embrace.

But as Alex went to move, he looked down and saw the earth had swallowed him up to his knees. He was held tightly, imprisoned in its grip.

Natasha reached out even further, and a puzzled expression replaced her beautiful smile. She was hurt—wounded—that he did not come to meet her. Tears fell from each eye. She brought both of her arms over her chest and embraced herself. She turned her back toward Alex and walked past the waterfall, disappearing from sight.

"Natasha! No! Come back. No," Alex cried.

The waterfall's song intensified the loneliness that devoured him.

"Roll Tide. Time to get up folks," Ron said, his head poking inside the tent. His arm entered next with a battery-powered lantern in his hand. He set it down and disappeared back outside.

Alex felt the weight of sadness lift as his dream dissolved into his foreign surroundings. His eyes came to focus on the lantern, and it took him a second to gather his thoughts and piece together where he was.

Others began to stir, some with moans of protest. This would be but the first of many mornings to wake in a strange location, not knowing what challenges the new day would bring.

Susan was awake, staring blankly at the ceiling. She was not a morning person. Alex had learned to keep conversations to a minimal until she had her first of many cups of coffee. Ask too many questions too early and risk getting your head bit off your shoulders.

Memories of the recent dream cascaded over him in waves. He remembered Natasha in her innocence—in her glory—and felt the magnetic urge to cling to her side. To join her and become one, for now, and all eternity.

Susan coughed, and then blew her nose in a tissue. Spoiling all the hope Natasha represented. Reminding Alex he was trapped—up to his knees in the earth—unable to pursue true love.

Matt, directly on the opposite end of Alex, turned on the lantern next to him, and was the first to rise and dress. He kept his back to everyone as he slipped off the pants he slept in and replaced them with the ones chosen for the journey. Modesty was a luxury not to be found this trip.

Logan peeled himself from the sleeping bag and let out a big yawn loud enough to wake most anyone from a dead sleep. He looked over at Natasha, who had propped herself up on her elbows.

She gave Logan a *go to hell stare*. "You snore."

"Me? I wasn't the only one snoring."

"Yeah, but yours has an annoying rasp that gets on my nerves."

Matt turned around and buttoned the front of his shirt. "Man, I was out from the time my head hit the pillow. I didn't hear anything last night. The sleeping bag could have had a little more cushion, but other than that, I had a good night."

Alex watched Susan rise and amble over to her bag. She pulled out a few items of clothing, shed her bed shirt and replace it with one made of denim, and quickly stepped into pants, pulling them up and buttoning them.

He was surprised Susan didn't wait for everyone else to dress and leave before exiting the security of her sleeping bag. She had always been on the shy side when it came to displaying her body. She only owned one-piece bathing suits, becoming incensed when Alex used to suggest she buy a bikini. *I guess the game we play now is just pretend no one else is in the room and get dressed as quickly as possible.*

Natasha followed Logan over by their bags and changed into the clothes of the day.

Matt let his gaze linger a bit too long when Natasha pulled her nightshirt off. She didn't notice, but Alex did. And Matt caught Alex taking notice. He responded by turning his gaze to the ground as he headed out the tent.

When Alex looked over at Natasha, she had turned his way and was buttoning her shirt. Her big brown eyes gazed right through him. Sleep still held the soft features of her face in its hold. Recognition didn't show in her eyes. He might as well have been a piece of furniture. The loneliness of the dream draped over him once more.

Susan had a brush in her hand, working out the kinks from her hair. It was as if no one else was in the tent but her.

The trip so far hadn't gone like he had imagined. What a fool he had been for thinking he and Natasha would be like two young lovers, hiding from the watchful eyes of the overseers. Stealing kisses, sharing furtive glances and touches. Where had his head been all that time? Up his ass?

Enough time wasted, he pulled himself out the sleeping bag, went to his bag next to Susan's, and started to dress.

Ben snored, rattling like Darth Vader with a stuffed nose.

"Hey, Ben. Ben. Wake up," Alex said, looping a belt through his jeans.

The athletic guy swallowed in mid-snore and opened his eyes.

"Time to get up, Ben. What gives? You're usually the first in line," Alex said.

"Yeah, but I'm always the last out of bed. It's a tradeoff I've learned to live with."

"We're going to the bathroom. We'll meet in the mess tent," Logan said. He put his hand on Natasha's shoulder and let her lead the way out the tent.

"That said, now that I'm awake, everyone needs to get out of my way." Ben pulled the sleeping bag top aside. While remaining flat on his back, he put his hands on the floor above his shoulders, and with a mighty display of physical prowess, lifted is legs, and sprang from the floor to land squarely on his feet.

Alex watched awestruck, feeling his manhood diminish. Youth was the most valuable possession a human would ever own.

Ben scurried to his bag and began dressing.

Natasha only glanced up from the floor as she reached the doorway. Not a smile, not a frown, just total indifference thrown Alex's way. At this point, he thought a heartfelt *fuck you* from her lips would make him feel better. Invoking any emotion would at least make it seem like she had some emotional investment in him.

"I'm going to the bathroom, too. Meet you at the mess tent," Susan said after placing the brush back in her bag. She was out the tent without once looking back.

After tying his shoes, Ben exited right on Susan's heels.

Alex was alone. Darkness edged the dim lighting of the small temporary enclosure, boxing him in. His life was boxed in, too. There was only one way out of the tent. Now, it became exceedingly obvious there was only one way for him to escape the bitter cage surrounding his life.

*

"I'll take that, little missy," Ron said as he took Natasha's gear from her and loaded it into the Warthog's rear cabin. She was first in line of the college crew. The others waited patiently behind her, with Alex bringing up the rear.

The smaller vehicle, the Mule, was no longer attached to the rear cabin, and was several yards away. Don hurriedly prepped it for departure.

The orange glow of the rising morning sun reflected off the snowcapped mountains picketing the western horizon. The mighty giants had served as sentries for millions of years. By fate or fortune, Mother Nature had decided to open the door for man to get a glimpse of what she created before the devastating asteroid bombardment some 65 million years ago. Times final gift was about to be shared.

Alex often wondered what path evolution might have taken had the dinosaurs not been destroyed. Bipedal dinosaurs were common, and if the creatures had flourished, might they have advanced into the sentient beings man had become? Of course, to progress as such, the tail would have to go. Arm length would have to grow too.

A funny thought crossed Alex's mind: reptilian men with short arms playing football and basketball. Life would be so much different if the evolutionary tree had branched differently. As it was, mammals evolved from reptiles, and then from small furry creatures into the mostly hairless, 46 chromosome species of ape.

"Morning, Ron. The special diet MREs—the ones we brought with us on the Chinook. Did you get those packed onboard?" Alex asked.

"Sure thing, Professor," Ron said.

"Susan has a peanut allergy, and we can't take any chances. They're in a white bag so you can't mistake them for other MREs," Alex said. He handed his bag to Ron and followed the others by the Warthog.

Natasha stepped carefully up the short ladder leading past the large tracks that would bring them to the destination. Matt held his hands at the ready as if to catch her if she fell. The big man, called Meat, was by the open door to the front cabin, a hand extended ready to assist. Chief waited by the foot of the ladder, his hands crossed behind his back.

Everyone carried jackets as the trip past the mountains would be a cold one, but the weather was too warm now to wear. One by one, his crew boarded the Warthog.

Chief hid behind his sunglasses, his stoic expression softened when Susan arrived at the ladder. "Good morning, Mrs. Klasse."

"Good morning, Chief," Susan said. She put her foot on the first step, and then turned her attention back to him. "Please, call me Susan."

Chief's head shifted to the side in a polite nod. He then turned his gaze to Alex. "Ready for the big adventure?"

Alex was a little surprised by Chiefs friendly tone. The man carried himself as all business and no pleasure. The only other time he seemed to warm up is when he spoke to Susan—which Alex noticed, but really didn't give a damn about. Hell, if Chief wanted her, he could have her! "I'd be lying if I didn't say I felt like a kid on Christmas morning. The wait has been excruciating. The day is finally here. Once we cross those mountains, there's a big old present just begging to be unwrapped."

Chief removed his sunglasses; it was too early in the morning for them to do him any good anyway. His eyes widened, and his face brightened. "You know, I've been on nearly a hundred missions in my career, but I've never felt like I do now. This one's different. I don't feel like a paid assassin. I feel like an explorer. Don't misunderstand me, I'm a professional soldier, and I'm proud of my work. This mission allows me to be something more than a harbinger of death and destruction. I can be part of a historical moment. You know, when I was a kid, I was fascinated by dinosaurs. I had coloring books, watched movies, and had picture books. My favorite toys were those little plastic figures. I had dinosaurs and Army men. I'd make death scenes with the dinosaurs always winning. Sometimes, when my older sister was in school, I'd set up T-rex and some other raptors eating one of her Barbie dolls. That used to piss her off big time."

Alex chuckled. It was common for young boys to have a fascination with dinosaurs. And that boyish fascination shone through the rugged façade of the harden mercenary now. "Chief, let's go make history."

"You got it, buddy." Chief patted Alex on the shoulder.

Alex ascended the short steps into the front cabin. Bench seats lined each side. His crew sat together on one side. Meat, Caveman, Suge, and Bats sat opposite on the other. Ron was in the cab at the wheel. Coop rode shotgun, his fingers tapping a keyboard on a laptop affixed to the dash.

His crew sat in the same order as they entered, with Natasha at one end and Susan on the other, closest to him. There was plenty of room on both sides, so he wouldn't be forced to sit with the Redwater bunch. In fact, at least another six people could fit without it being cramped.

Coop looked over at Alex, nodding as he steadily typed. He then pulled his hands away from the keyboard, hit one last key, rose from his seat, and entered the cabin. "Everyone enjoy breakfast?"

"I know I did," Alex said, amongst affirmations from his crew. "The maple sausage patty was delicious. The oatmeal and dried fruit too."

"I didn't realize your wife had a nut allergy until Ron mentioned it this morning. I hope that's not going to complicate matters any," Coop said.

"She'll be fine. We brought enough food to last six weeks. We also have antihistamines and some Epi-Pens. Susan knows what to be cautious of when it comes to food," Alex said. "One thing's for sure, you guys eat better than I do when I go on my trips in the States. Which usually is peanut butter, potted meat or Vienna Sausages, or some combination of the three."

"The food's not too bad. You'll get tired of it soon enough, though. We've stocked a variety of MREs and freeze-dried products. MREs in general don't have a lot of fiber and do have a lot of salt. Which means you need to drink plenty of water, or you'll get constipated. Eat at least one of the fiber bars a day."

"What about toilet paper? Do we have to go third world country and use our left hand to wipe?" Ben asked.

Coop laughed. "You can if you want. There is a limited amount of paper towels for us to use as we need. Once we cross the mountains, there'll be other natural resources at our disposal. I suggest you wipe carefully."

"I've never wiped my ass with a dinosaur foot before. This is gonna be fun," Caveman joked.

Natasha timidly raised a hand. "So, uh, how often are we going to stop, you know...to go to the bathroom?"

Bats had a pocketknife out and shaved callouses from around his fingers. His gaze focused on his work. "Just like a woman. Gotta stop at every truck stop on the way to take a piss."

Alex winced and almost said something to the man, but thought it not to be the appropriate time for a lesson in gender sensitivity.

Natasha looked stunned at first and blushed. But then her bottom lip tightened, and she narrowed her eyes, not looking the least bit pleased.

"The terlit is right over there." Caveman pointed toward the rear.

Natasha leaned forward and looked where he directed. "There's no toilet there. There's not even a door."

"See that five gallon bucket?" Caveman asked.

"Yeah, so?" Natasha said.

"So when you gotta go, you can piss in there."

"You're not serious..." Natasha stiffened, apparently realizing he was serious.

"Okay, look," Coop spread his hands, "we're about to leave. I'm figuring an eight-hour drive—twelve at the most. The terrain will be tricky, and we need to be careful. There's no Triple A out here to give us a tow. We will stop every couple of hours, mainly for vehicle inspection. More if we need to. Everyone should try to regulate your body functions to coincide. That said, if anyone can't wait, the bucket is open." Coop returned to his seat wearing a wide grin across his lips.

Alex wasn't sure if Coop smiled because of the shock value of his comment or if the man was as eager to begin the journey as he was.

CHAPTER 9

The Warthog slowly rose up an incline and then suddenly dipped, jarring Natasha's head. The three-hour ride hadn't been as bad as she feared. The seats weren't any more comfortable than on the Chinook, and it was only times like these when she wished she had a fatter ass. For this trip, a Kardashian bottom would suit her nicely.

Don drove the Mule several yards in front of the Warthog, testing the path first. The fissure served as a natural road and varied in depth and width. There was a time or two when he had to use the blade on the front end to widen the path, but width was usually not a problem. What scared Natasha the most was when the Warthog tipped to one side or the other. Once, the incline was so great, the vehicle slid sideways. She feared it would turn over. Fortunately, the tracks found purchase on the earth and continued on the path.

She was starting to feel more comfortable around the Redwater crew, although none of them bothered to engage her group in conversation. Suge and Caveman played games on their phones, Bats slowly sharpened his knife, Meat doodled away in his notebook, and Chief sat silently, his arms crossed. With the dark glasses on she couldn't tell if he were awake or not.

Alex was reading something on his ePad, Susan had her book, and Logan typed away on his phone, writing in his journal, she guessed. Ben had his crossword puzzles, and Matt...Matt was looking her way. His happy expression seemed contrived.

Bored, it just seemed silly to waste time playing on her phone. Who were these men? They were going to be together for the next several weeks, now was as good a time as any to get to know them better.

"Excuse me." Natasha leaned forward, Suge sat directly across from her. "Your name is Henry, right?"

Suge darted his gaze at her, and returned to his phone, thumbs a-blazing on the keypad. "That's me," he said, his tone pleasant.

"Would you prefer I call you Henry, or is it okay to call you Suge? Chief said we had to ask if we can call you Suge."

"Sure, you can call me Suge." He looked up from the phone and shoved it in his front pocket.

"How about me? Can I call you Suge?" Ben asked.

By this time everyone, except Bats, had turned away from what they were doing, their attention now on the conversation at hand.

"Suge's fine. In fact, everyone can call me Suge."

Mutters of thanks and head nods came from the college crew.

"And thank you for asking," Suge said, sounding genuinely pleased.

Logan fidgeted in his seat, and then sighed loudly.

Okay, this is working, Natasha thought. Before she had a chance to continue, Ben interrupted.

"Hey, uh, Bats," Ben said.

The man dragged his knife blade across a ceramic rod and stopped. His eyes looked up from under his cap. "Yeah, what can I do you for?"

"I've been wondering something since Chief introduced you. Oh, I love your Texas accent, by the way. I've always wanted to visit Texas. I see all kind of barbecue joints on TV I'd like to hit up. Anyway, I was wondering—about your nickname. Bats, you a big Batman fan?"

The question hung in the air for what became several uncomfortable moments. The blade continued to pass across the ceramic rod again. "No. I'm not a fan of some fuck-tard who wears a mask and parades around in tights."

"Oh, yeah. I get it. Well, why do they call you *Bats*, then?" Ben asked.

"Simple, they call me Bats because of my medical condition."

"Medical condition? You have trouble seeing?"

"No, I've been diagnosed as bat-shit crazy."

"It's true. I'm the doctor that gave him that name," Caveman said. "Don't worry though. He gets along just fine as long as he gets his medicine."

"Glad to hear that," Ben said, and settled into his seat. He turned his head and watched Bats from the corner of his eye.

"Yep, as long as Bats here gets to kill something every three or four days, he's as happy as a dung beetle in a cow field," Caveman said.

Logan squirmed in his seat some more and arched his back.

Matt asked, "Hey, Logan, you okay?"

"Yeah. I'll be all right. I just have to hold it for another hour," Logan said.

"You gotta pee? Use the bucket," Caveman said.

"Uh, no, thank you. I'll hold it."

"What's the matter? Your peter too small to reach the bucket?" Caveman asked.

"No, I—"

"Aw, come on. Everyone pees and poos. Ain't none of us here ain't never seen a dick before. Grow a set and whip it out. There's more room out than in," Caveman said.

Challenging Logan's manhood didn't set well with him. He looked like he was about to explode, but then checked himself, closed his eyes, apparently in hopes of composing himself. "I would rather just wait and maintain some dignity and—"

"Dignity?" Bats said, freezing the blade near the middle of the ceramic rod. "What's the matter, boy? You think you're better than us?"

"I didn't say that. If I'd rather wait to use the bathroom, that's my business. I can take care of myself." Logan leaned forward, his gaze firmly directed on Bats.

"You know, I thought there was something different about you." Bats brought a thumb over to the blade and brushed it against the sharp edge. "You squat when you pee, boy?"

Logan stiffened his back, balling both fists. "What if I did? It's none of your fucking business."

Alex rose from his seat as if he were about to intervene. The Warthog violently shook, sending him to his knees.

"What's happening?" Susan shrieked.

At first Natasha thought the Warthog was in the process of rolling over but realized that it only rocked back and forth—spilling everyone off the benches.

"Earthquake! Hang on," Coop cried from the cab.

Objects clanged against the side of the Warthog, which had now come to a stop. Curses and various cries of surprise exploded from the riders.

Natasha had never been in an earthquake before and didn't know what to expect. Her mind ran wild with an image of the ground cracking open, like in the movie *The Day After Tomorrow*, with the vehicles falling down a deep abyss and swallowed by the Earth's core.

Something large hit the roof. Now she feared half the mountain would fall on top and bury them in a ton of rubble. They would either suffocate or starve to death. The Warthog would serve as one large coffin for the 13 would-be explorers.

The rumbling slowly subsided, and the earth stopped shifting. Natasha was on her side, and her arms covered her head. She lifted her gaze, and saw members of the team slowly pull themselves from the floor, exploring body parts with fingers, searching for possible injury.

Logan and Bats rose to their feet, their noses inches away, gazes locked. Bats still had the knife in his hand. Neither flinched.

"Anybody hurt?" Coop leaned out the cab, rubbing the back of his neck.

"Bats, everyone, take your seats and wait for orders," Chief commanded.

The Texan turned toward his leader and sat on the bench. He closed his knife and put the sharpener in his pocket.

Alex helped Susan up. "Guys, everyone okay?" He turned his gaze to Natasha.

"I'm okay . . . I think." Pain in her left elbow indicated one point of impact. She rubbed her fingers on it and felt peeled skin and a slight wetness from blood. "Just skinned up a bit," she said, and rose.

"Here, I'll get a Band-Aid." Matt maneuvered past those still standing to the medical cabinet on the wall. He returned with an antibacterial wipe and an adhesive bandage.

"I'm fine," Ben said. He picked up his crossword book and sat next to Logan.

The Redwater crew sat ready to spring into action, their attention focused solely on Chief.

"I think we're okay," Alex said to Coop. "What's it look like out there? How bad is it?"

"All I know is that it could be worse. There's nothing much between us and Don. He's okay—stuck his arm out the window and gave me a thumb-up. There's a big boulder in front of him, though. We're going to have to go outside and take a look," Coop said. "It's twenty-two degrees outside. You'll need jackets."

"Hee-hee, I love me some cold weather," Caveman said. "I can layer up and stay warm. In the summer, I can't take enough off to get cool."

Chief had moved by the door. He tried to open it, but it wouldn't budge. "Can't leave from here. We're going to have to go out the hatch."

Meat grabbed the ladder and his jacket. He placed the ladder under the hatch, stepped up, and opened it.

Cool air drifted into the cabin, tickling the inside of Natasha's nose. Matt had wiped her small scrape and just then finished applying the bandage.

"Better?" Matt asked.

"Yes, thanks." She followed Matt over to the bench, where everyone busily slipped arms through jacket sleeves.

The Redwater crew filed through the hatch first.

Alex stepped up the ladder and poked his upper body through the opening. After several seconds, he said, "Everyone follow me." He disappeared from the cabin, but then his hand dropped through the hatch. "Come on, Susan."

Susan complied. Ben was next, and then Logan.

Matt insisted that Natasha go before him. Alex's hand reached through the opening, his smiling face peered down from above. The magic still danced in his eyes. She placed her fingers in his cool hand and felt the thrill of his touch. Sweet memories of the intimate times spent together pushed against the wall of resentment. She loved this man. Gave herself to him like no other. He made her feel things both physically and spiritually beyond what she thought were possible.

As Natasha rose above the opening, Alex asked, "How are you feeling?"

He worded the question in such a way she knew he was asking more that if she were just hurt from the fall. He was asking her feelings about him. There was no doubt the vibes she had been sending to him were negative. Alex sensed it, and she knew that he knew the trouble in their strained relationship had to be resolved. "I'll be okay."

"I hope and pray that you will. Better pull your hood up and get the gloves from your pocket. It's cold out here."

"Thanks, I will," Natasha said, and made room for Matt to come through.

Once the associate professor was out, Alex said to him, "Join the others on the ground. I'll be right behind you."

Matt looked over at Natasha and then back at Alex, furrowing his brow.

"I don't want her aggravating her injury. This is a high point, and she can keep an eye on things. Or if we need something from the cabin, she's right there to get it for us."

"Oh, okay," Matt said, and shrugged. He maneuvered over to the ladder leading down the side of the cabin to the ground.

"You don't have to protect me. I can take care of myself," Natasha said after she was sure Matt was clear of earshot.

"I know that you can," Alex said, winked, and headed down the ladder to join with the others.

Natasha scanned the surroundings. The giant mountains to either side made her feel more claustrophobic than being inside the Warthog. As fate would have it, the pathway had narrowed, and a huge boulder set several yards in front of the Mule, totally blocking passage. Other large rocks and boulders lined ridges on the mountains, threatening to fall. Things were not looking good for the home team.

On one side of the Warthog, where the door was located, rubble had slid down the mountain and piled up. A few of the Redwater gang were looking that over, assessing the situation.

Coop and the rest of the expedition had ambled over to the boulder. He and Chief were in deep discussion. Susan huddled next to Alex nearby.

Natasha was on the outside looking in again. She knew Alex meant well by leaving her up there, but it only fueled the growing fire of bitterness. Something had to give—sooner than later.

Don left the boulder and got inside the Mule. He fired it up, the crowd in front of the boulder parted, and he came to a stop a few feet away. The boulder was slightly larger than the Mule. There was no way that thing could push the massive rock out of the way.

Suge double-timed to the Warthog's rear cabin and went inside. He came out with a roll of thick electrical cable on his shoulder, a strange pair of goggles on his forehead, and a weird contraption held in his hands. Somebody had a plan, and Natasha hoped it would work.

Matt headed back toward the Warthog and climbed his way back up. "Hey," he said.

"What are we doing?" she asked.

"They're going to use a laser on the boulder, try to drill some holes in it, and see if it will break into smaller pieces. Ron's going to fire up the Warthog and see if we can pull away from the mess on the right side."

"What happens if that doesn't work?"

"Coop said they had some explosives that could blow the boulder to pieces, but he's afraid of starting an avalanche. We can't exactly back up from where we are right now."

"I guess not," Natasha said.

The two watched Suge get a lift from his buddies and climb on top of the boulder. Don plugged the electrical cord into an outlet on the front of the vehicle. Not long after, Suge had his goggles on and pointed the laser at the top of the boulder. Slight wisps of smoke rose among the steady hum of the Mule's nuclear powered engine.

A half hour passed, Suge shut down the laser, and pulled the goggles to his forehead.

Ben had been watching the whole time. Coop said something to him, and he ran toward the Warthog.

When he arrived, Natasha called down, "What's going on?"

"They cut five holes about an inch wide through the boulder. Coop says the boulder is made of intrusive igneous rock, which means it has coarse grains, and though hard as shit, it's brittle as shit, too. He sent me to get some water."

"Water?" she said.

"Yeah, we're going to pour the water in the holes. The water will turn to ice and expand. It should break the boulder apart."

"Wow. I would have never thought of that," Natasha said as Ben went to the rear cabin and came back with two containers of water.

Natasha looked over at Matt. "Do you'll think it'll work?"

"Well, if it doesn't, they'll probably put in explosives and hope for the best.

*

It would take several hours for the water to turn to ice. Ron had successfully driven the Warthog away from the debris blocking the door and had parked behind the Mule.

The crew used the time to eat, and then broke off into smaller groups. Three of the Redwater team started a poker game. Ben wanted to play, and became such an annoyance, they let him in the game just to shut him up.

Matt sat next to Natasha and ran his mouth ninety-to-nothing.

Susan read her book, and Alex was outside with Chief, Coop, and the rest of the Redwater team.

Logan was alone. He was used to being alone, in fact. It was his choice not to join the others. Part of his youth's defensive mechanism carried to this day. Being an introvert wasn't a good or bad thing. It's just what and who he was.

The front cabin door opened. "Hey guys, gear up, and come see," Alex's said.

Everyone stopped what they were doing, put on jackets, and headed out.

Coop waited by the boulder. From the looks of things, his plan had worked. The boulder had large cracks on the outside surface. Chunks here and there had broken off. The Mule could easily push the smaller pieces aside. Still, though, the bulk of the boulder remained.

"I wish we had a jackhammer, but we don't. It would take too long to hammer and chisel this boulder down to size. So, what I need are a few volunteers to climb up the side of that mountain."

Coop pointed at a ledge some thirty feet high. Rocks of various sizes piled along the edge. "If we could toss some of those rocks and hit the boulder, the impact should break it into pieces small enough for the Mule to push out of the way."

Logan's gaze followed the side of the mountain. The ledge poked out just about directly over the boulder. Fortunately, to the left side of the ledge, the mountain sloped, and had enough handholds and smaller ridges to stand on to where he thought he could make it.

"All we need is a few volunteers," Coop said.

"I'll do it. I've been climbing before. That actually doesn't look too difficult," Logan said, and pulled the cuff of his gloves, snugging in his fingers.

"I'm in," Ben said, and stepped over by Logan.

"I like heights. Makes me feel like I'm flying," Bats said, and then stretched out his arms and cracked his knuckles.

"Logan, you and Ben be careful . . . uh, you too, Bats," Alex said.

"Sure thing," Logan said. He turned and headed to the edge of the fissure.

"You better let me lead," Bats said. "I don't want you falling down and knocking me off the mountain."

Logan stopped and looked back at Bats, who steadily approached. If the mercenary was trying to get him to lose his cool, it wasn't going to work. This mission was too important and this task too risky to start a pissing match. "Go ahead. With a name like Bats, if you fall, I'm sure you'll be able to just flap your arms and fly away." He wanted to add, *or crazy enough to believe you can*, but didn't.

Bats passed him without saying a word and began his ascent, taking firm holds and climbing without a moment of hesitation. This was not the man's first scurry up a mountain slope.

Logan waited for Bats to move over from a direct line of fire, and asked Ben, "You want to go next?"

"Okay. Race you to the top." Ben began his climb, using the same path that Bats had before.

Logan followed at the appropriate time, and without any drama, the three reached the ledge.

The crew below had moved well away from the boulder. Several gave a wave when Logan peered over the side of the ledge. He waved back, and then turned and saw Ben and Bats looking over the inventory of rocks. The ledge itself was a good ten feet wide, but some of the rubble was piled in a way that it had to be avoided. Some had to be walked on, which made shifting rocks a slipping possibility.

Ben grabbed hold of a large rock and tried to pick it up. "Damn. This thing's heavy." The rock looked a couple of feet tall and about as wide. The athlete stepped away. "I could probably lift it if it was balanced. I bet it weighs over two hundred pounds."

"We'll just have to work together," Logan said. "Won't we, Bats?"

The man pointed out a rock to Ben. "Let's get to work."

The rock was smaller than the one Ben had chosen. The two maneuvered to either side and lifted it in unison.

"Wait a minute," Logan said. He hurriedly kicked and moved some smaller debris out of their path to the edge.

"Coming through," Ben said as Logan stepped off to the side.

"On three," Bats said. "One . . . two . . . three."

The rock left their hands and plummeted through the air, striking the boulder dead center. It crashed with a dull thump and scattering debris. About a third of the boulder sheared away from the large mass. The crew below hooped and hollered.

"Good shot, guys. Coop really knows his stuff. A few more like that and we'll be done," Logan said.

The next two rocks didn't produce the same results, but the third one knocked off another good chunk. Logan waited for one of the men to tire, and then he'd get his turn too.

On the way to get another rock, Ben's foot shifted, twisting his ankle. He hit the ground. "Ouch. Shit."

"You okay?" Logan asked.

"I think so." Ben slowly rose and tested out his ankle. "Yeah. I'm good. Just sprained a bit."

"Let me take over. You need to save your ankle for the climb back down," Logan said.

Ben nodded, and moved out of the way, still testing his ankle.

"I'm following your lead," Logan said to Bats.

"That one over there," he said.

They came to the rock, one of many of near the same size. Bats positioned himself to one side and found a finger-hold on the bottom.

"Careful of the edge. I wouldn't want you to fall," Logan said. The edge of that side of the ledge was less than two feet away. A deep crevice cut the side of the mountain directly underneath. From the looks of it, it might have been over a hundred feet deep.

"I don't need no Twinkie telling be to be careful. Shut up and lift," Bats said.

Rage swelled inside Logan, fighting to get out. He thought how easy it would be right now to shove that son-of-a-bitch and send him head over heels over the edge to his death. Bats would have to confess to St. Peter that a *Twinkie* got the best of him.

He shook off the feeling. The people counting on him to come through were more important. His fingers went underneath the rock, and the two men lifted. The rock was heavy. A lot heavier than he thought it would be. And from the expression on Bats' face, heavier than he expected too.

Bats stuck his left foot backward, as if to keep from falling off balance. The ledge crumbled underneath, sending him downward.

The rock dipped from Bats' side, and Logan quickly pulled his fingers from harm's way as it crashed to the ground.

When he looked over, Bats was gone.

"Bats!" Logan yelled, and then dropped to his knees and crawled near the edge. To his amazement, there was enough of the jagged rocky edge for Bats to get a hand on.

"Ben! Get over here!" Logan called. He laid on his stomach and reached a hand toward the mercenary. The hope of rescue was a good foot short.

"Go away. I got this," Bats said, voice straining.

"Like hell you do, asshole! Ben, hold my legs." Logan felt Ben's arms grab tightly around his thighs, and he maneuvered his hand over by Bats', grabbing his wrist. "I can't pull you up. You'll have to use your other hand to grab my arm. You're going to have to use me as a ladder."

The man didn't protest. His right hand came up and grabbed Logan's arm.

The additional 200 pounds plus threatened to yank Logan's arm from the socket. He let go of Bats' wrist. The man pulled himself up and grabbed on Logan's jacket. Logan began to slide, and he couldn't help but cry out in pain, his chest mashing against the rocky ledge.

Bats wasted no time, making moves, catching quick breaths in between, until he finally found himself at the top, where he rolled over on the ledge and heaved for air.

The deep crevice passed from Logan's sight as Ben pulled him to safety. The small of his back cooled with frigid air; his shirt and jacket had been pulled away during Bats' climb. His ribs ached, and his right arm felt like a limp noodle.

"Damn, that was close. How you doing, Bats?" Ben picked himself up and brushed off.

"I'm . . . I'm good," he said.

"Logan?" Ben said.

"I'm a little bruised up. My arm went through a lot of trauma. I'll be okay," Logan said. He had one foot and one knee on the ground, working his arm and shoulder. Ben offered his left hand, he took it, and stood.

Bats was up and brushed himself off. "I'm good. I'm good," he said, as if trying to convince himself. "We need to finish what we started." He stepped over to another rock, well away from the ledge. He turned his gaze up to Ben and Logan.

"I can do this. My ankle's all right. Move over to the side, Logan, and we'll handle this," Ben said.

In no condition to argue, Logan moved out of the way, and peered down at the crowd. Every neck craned upward. Surely they had seen the near disaster, and if any had cried out during the event, he was too caught up to notice. He lifted a thumb, jabbing it back and forth in the air.

Ben and Bats reached the edge with another rock. The missile left their fingers and found its target, further reducing the boulder to a manageable size.

CHAPTER 10

The Warthog's engine hummed as the massive mountain range steadily shrank in its wake. Coop's plan had worked. The Mule successfully powered through the shattered remains of the boulder, clearing the path. It wasn't long after the terrain took a downward angle and gave Alex hope that the finish line was within their grasps.

Fate was kind to the interlopers. The two vehicles trudged along the natural path without any other hazards threatening along the way. The trip past the mountains had taken nearly ten hours. And now they traveled on pristine land; land that no human had ever set foot before.

Fatigue had set in, tightening the muscles on Alex's back and neck. He wanted to stretch, but Susan leaned into one side of him, her head on his shoulder while she dozed.

Chief, who had formal medical training, had made a sling for Logan's arm. Logan had protested but gave in, and commented afterward that supporting his arm made his shoulder feel better. Near as they could tell, time and Advil would be the cure.

Bats was lucky to be alive. It was quick thinking on Logan's part that had saved the man. Alex wondered what was going on now in Bats' mind. He was so close to death, literally clinging to life by the tips of his fingers with certain doom mere seconds away. Whatever it was, Alex certainly couldn't tell by reading his face. Bats had assumed his faraway stare and scraped blade against sharpener, keeping his secrets to himself.

Coop rose from his seat and poked his head from the cab. "Night's approaching. The Warthog has lights and low-level radar, but we have no plans of traveling at night unless there's an emergency situation. Ron's about to pull us over, and we'll set up camp."

Susan stirred at Coop's announcement. She cleared her throat and wiped her mouth with an unsteady hand. "Good. I'm ready to get out of this thing. I hope—good grief! What's that smell?"

Caveman grinned and gave her a wink. "Uh, that would be me."

"Damn, man, you couldn't have waited another five minutes and fart outside?" Suge said.

"I done told you, there's more room out than there is in," Caveman said.

"John, show the ladies here a little respect," Chief said, and turned his gaze toward Susan.

Natasha held her nose, and Logan had lifted the front of his tee shirt up under his eyes to use as a filter. Matt shook his head in disbelief.

"I owe you one," Ben said, exaggerated revenge in his tone.

"Don't start nothing you can't finish, big boy," Caveman said, apparently eager for the competition.

The Warthog slowed and stopped. "We're here. Roll Tide," Ron announced from the cab.

*

It was much warmer outside than it was in the Warthog's front cabin. Alex hadn't realized that at one point the heater kicked off, with the air conditioning switching in to maintain the temperature. For such an industrial looking machine, the Warthog was finely tuned for creature comforts.

It was barely light outside. It was a bit shocking to look up and see the misty dome that surrounded the foreign land. The cold mountain air mixed with the rising heat of the earth creating a phenomena unlike any other. Alex wondered if something else was involved in forming the dome. Perhaps something within the gases belching from the volcano; he noticed the sulphur odor had diminished, but he could still taste it on the back of his tongue. Either his sense of smell had grown accustomed to it, or the chemicals had desensitized his olfactory nerves. Whatever, he hoped the effects wouldn't linger after returning home.

The stars, for the brief time he gazed upward back at the camp the previous night, had looked magnificent. No man-made light pollution to block the view of the universe. There would be no star gazing for the remaining of this trip.

Everyone was eager to assist in setting up for the night. Ron had parked the Warthog in a flat area with low vegetation—scrubby grasses of some sort. About 50 yards away a forest grew thick. There was no way they'd be traveling through it, although he imagined the Mule would stand a much better chance over the Warthog. Even from the distance the trees looked massive, spreading out their leafy canopies, blurring the arms of one tree into the next.

The Redwater crew took the lead and started unloading the rear cabin. Don strung a few lights around the perimeter and plugged them into the Mule's power outlets. Bats and Suge rolled out the waterproof canopy that ran the length of the front cabin by the door. It might have been possible for everyone to sleep inside the cabin, but no one would want to be packed in like sardines. Some would have to sleep outside of it.

Alex hoped that weather and indigenous life would treat them kindly. Indigenous life? Were any dinosaurs nocturnal? He didn't know. It only made sense that dinosaurs followed the same evolutionary path as other animal phylum. So there was probably more than one creature or two who would be on the hunt tonight.

As for his crew, basically everyone stood around waiting for a member of Redwater to give instructions. Alex felt like he was mostly in the way, and couldn't help but drift from the pack and stare into the distance in hope of catching a glimpse of a prehistoric behemoth wandering about the countryside.

Unexpectedly, a foreboding feeling that the whole trip had been a ruse and he had been played a fool wormed its way into his mind. *What if* the picture was faked? Allegedly, there was a video of the pterosaur. He had never seen it. *What if* Ace Corporation contrived an elaborate plan and waited for a sucker to raise his hand in order to take advantage of him? And if this had all been a bundle of lies and deceit, what else wasn't he aware of? Now he considered the possibility of being in danger by the very group sent to protect them.

A needlelike pain jabbed Alex's forearm. His hand instinctually slapped the area and came back with a streak of brown smear across his palm.

Coop walked by his side. "We've got some insect spray in rear cabin. Be sure all of your crew uses it, even the ones who are going to sleep in the front cabin. I know we've all had our shots, but there is a lot of unknown out here."

"I'll be sure to do that. Did you bring any dinosaur repellant? I don't see signs of any kind of life other than flying insects," Alex said.

"I've already told you we didn't expect to see much life on the outlining areas. We certainly don't want to put ourselves deeper in country at this point. We're tired and need to be fresh for an encounter, if we can help it."

Alex shifted his gaze to the ground and slowly shook his head. "I . . . don't know. I'm starting to feel like we're on a hunt to find a pot of gold at the end of a rainbow—like finding dinosaurs still alive is just a big fantasy. When I look around I'm seeing reality— the only reality I've known. And . . . and it's hard for me to wrap my mind around seeing a prehistoric beast in this reality. Is . . . there something else going on about the mission that you're not telling me?"

"Alex, I'm not sure what you expected to see when you've been on your other *strange creature* hunts. But I know you didn't find anything, or the whole world would know of it. Maybe you're subconsciously expecting the same results here. You know the mission. There's nothing else to add. It's been a rough day. We'll be eating soon, and then we'll get some rest. The low-level radar and thermal cameras are operational, and we'll get an alert if any *visitors* happen upon us."

Coop was either one of the straightest shooters Alex had ever met or the master of deceivers. He liked the man. He *wanted* to like the man and hoped to goodness nothing would change for him not to do so. "Yeah. I'm tired, anxious, and a lot of other things I'd rather not discuss. Thanks, Coop. You and the others did a great job getting us here."

"Tomorrow, we'll launch the drone. The good part's just getting started." After patting Alex on the shoulder, he headed back inside the front cabin.

By this time sides had gone up under the canopy, boxing in a nice sized area leading into the front cabin's entrance. Good timing, as the day's light faded faster than he had anticipated. It was time to join up with the others and complete the nightly rituals.

Alex walked from the front of the Warthog past the canopy, and saw Ron warming MREs on an electrical contraption plugged into the Warthog. Having a nuclear engine was wonderful, providing energy for all sorts of things.

A few crewmembers were in line at the rear cabin. Bats was in charge of handing out sleeping bags. Others already had their bag and were heading inside. From what he knew, he, Susan, Natasha, and Matt would be inside, along with Coop. The Redwater gang opted for the canopy area. Ben had said he wanted to stay outside, but Logan never made any commitment to where he would bunk for the night.

Logan was last in line as Alex neared. Bats waited to hand him his sleeping bag.

Alex stopped dead in his tracks. Something was up with Bats. His body language spoke volumes. Alex decided to hang back and let the two work things out, and step in only if the situation called for it.

Bats maintained that cold, long distance stare at Logan. He remained still as a statue and showed no emotion at all.

Alex saw Logan's jaw tightening, and after several moments, Logan said, "Is there a problem?"

"Earlier . . . I don't think I told you thanks for giving me a hand. So, thanks," Bats said.

Logan's stiff shoulders relaxed. "You're welcome. I'm sure you would have done the same for me."

"Maybe," Bats said. His brow crinkled like it was a scenario he played in his mind.

"So we're cool?" Logan said. The man obviously wanted to get past any bad blood between them. It would certainly help clear one of the unnecessary distractions on this trip.

"Yeah. We're cool. Just keep your hands to yourself, and there won't be any problems." Bats tried to give Logan his sleeping bag.

Logan raised his hands in frustration. "Bats, you are a man without a clue, which surprises me and frustrates me at the same time. You're older than I am—been all over the world and met people from different societies. You've seen and done things I've never imagined—lived a hard life I will never know. You'd think a man with your life's experiences would understand people better.

Know that not everybody thinks the same way—how some of us are put together different. Not in a bad way, just different from your way. You actually told me '*keep your hands to yourself.*' Do you know how ignorant that makes you look? You and I are different. You should have enough insight to know I'd never even consider *putting my hands on you.* I respect you for who and what you are, and in turn, I expect the same from you. So, my advice is to *get with the times.* Erase ancient stereotypes and unjustified prejudices of the past. Gay people aren't some monsters that can't resist molesting the same sex. We're just people. People like you. Just trying to live life and make it in this world. So I ask this, if you want to thank me for saving your life, you can do it by rethinking everything you know about people and their sexuality. Stop putting barriers between you and those who are different." He took his sleeping bag from Bats.

Alex watched Bats' face the whole time Logan lit into him. Bats' stoic demeanor hid whether the words penetrated callused perceptions or if a lit fuse was about to reach a pile of TNT. Logan had drawn a line in the sand and disarmed himself by taking the sleeping bag. It was Bats' move now.

Bats' head shifted to the side. With a raised lowered lip and a slight nod, he said, "I can do that."

*

With no stars shining from above or the yellow-orange light of the moon to give its hope, darkness surrounded the camp like a cage. Early man would build fires at night to keep roaming predators at bay. While no one took the time to gather wood to build a fire, the few lights Don set up acted as a substitute, crudely surrounding the perimeter.

Alex didn't know if his MRE, home-style chicken with noodles, tasted so good because it was a quality product or if it was because he was so hungry. The Warthog had plenty of snacks in the front cabin, but the rough ride on the way up made his stomach too queasy for him to care. He imagined he'd drop a few pounds over the next three weeks—a few pounds he certainly could spare. To drink, he chose a packet of lemon flavoring to zest up his water. No beer or wine for this trip. At least, a variety of flavorings, including tea and coffee, were available.

The rear cabin had a bladder holding a couple of hundred gallons of water. That wasn't nearly enough water to last the trip and wasn't meant to. There was plenty of water available in Patagonia, and they would have to resupply often. Contamination wouldn't be an issue, as the rear cabin housed a reverse osmosis water purifier. Still, water other than for drinking had to be rationed. Washcloth baths would have to suffice until they found a river or stream to bath in.

Everyone seemed in good spirits. The Redwater crew intermingled more with Susan and his students.

Natasha treated him like he was invisible, and Matt acted like he was tethered to her. The disturbing part—Natasha didn't seem to mind.

Logan mostly kept to himself, as if something weighed on his mind. For whatever reason, Alex didn't think it had anything to do with Logan's conflict with Bats.

Susan sat at a foldout table on one of the few foldout chairs brought on the trip. She sipped on instant coffee as Chief described in minute detail some of the more harrowing adventures he'd been on.

Ben finally had to put his money where his mouth was and took Caveman on in an arm wrestling match. At first, it had looked like Ben was going to win. As the back of Caveman's hand neared inches from the table, the big man grinned like the Cheshire Cat and easily reversed the situation, practically toppling Ben from his chair. At least Ben didn't get his arm broken.

The fatigue of the day had finally won. Coop declared lights out, and everyone nestled in their own small personal space. The Sandman played his enchanted song, weighing down eyelids with magical dust.

*

A sharp beep emitted from the Warthog's cab. Alex sprang up from his sleeping bag and looked around, trying to get his bearings.

Coop rose and flipped on a light. Everyone in the front cabin stirred.

"What is it?" Alex asked.

"It's the movement alarm. The low-level radar and thermal camera work together to give an alert when a life form is detected," Coop said as he entered the cabin.

Susan sat up. Her head swiveled about as she tried to focus. "Alex?"

"Everyone stay calm. Let Coop call the shots." Alex stepped over to the cab and looked over Coop's shoulder as he fiddled with a computer screen.

The image showed a mostly black screen with something on all fours passing by the area. From this view, it was hard to tell the size, but the shape was clear, although it looked cartoonish. The thermal image showed bright reds, greens, blues, and yellows—different colors in variance of heat from the creature.

"Hang on a second. I'll zoom a night vision camera on it." Coop clicked a few buttons and brought up another screen. The black and green picture showed a prehistoric creature of some type, ambling across the scrubby grass.

"Son-of-a-bitch," Alex marveled.

"Whatcha got, boss?" Meat had entered the front cabin. He was the first on watch duty tonight.

"Not sure, but it doesn't look that big. Did you see it out there?" Coop said.

"Thought I heard something, but I couldn't see anything. Do you want me to shoo it away?" Meat asked.

"No. Let's not make any contact if we don't have to. If he doesn't bother us, we won't bother him. Alex, do you know what this is?" Coop asked.

"I've been studying up on my dinosaurs. It looks a lot like . . . hold on." Alex went to his bag, pulled out his electronic pad, and turned it on. "Okay, that thing looks a little bigger than a sheep. See the back of the head? That's called a neck frill. And its mouth, the frontal beak? I'm pretty sure that's a Protoceratops."

"Easy for you to say," Meat joked.

"According to this, it had powerful jaw muscles and dozens of teeth. You wouldn't want to go sticking your hand near its mouth. Fortunately, it wasn't a meat eater. Still, I wouldn't take any chances. That thing weighs around four hundred pounds and could be a handful."

"Meat, go back outside and watch it through the night goggles. If it starts heading this way, fire a warning shot to spook it off. Don't, and I repeat *don't*, shoot at the thing," Coop said.

"Gotcha, boss." Meat disappeared from the front cabin.

"Can you get pictures of that?" Alex asked.

"It's all on video. In fact, it's being beamed up on satellite, and the boys at Ace Corp are watching it just like us."

By this time Susan and the others had crowded Alex from the backside, trying to get a look. Alex stepped away not to hog an experience of a lifetime. That was a dinosaur out there. An honest to goodness dinosaur! Euphoria washed over him as if he were baptized by Jesus himself and the Holy Spirit had imbued him with power. All those years of chasing after mythological beasts had only led to disappointment. This was real. This was now. This was a gift from time's past. He was there as one of the first witnesses.

"Looks like he's not interested in us. He's heading off toward the woods," Coop said as the animal's tail swayed behind him—as if giving a slow wave farewell.

Alex felt like he floated on air. When his crew turned to him, wearing wide smiles and amazed expressions, he was too excited to even talk.

He focused on Natasha. That loving expression had returned in her gaze. That look would inspire a thousand ships to leave for war. For him, it fueled a transformation, clearing his mind to see the future.

CHAPTER 11

It took nearly two hours for Alex and the others to calm down and get back to sleep. The rest of the night was uneventful. A cacophony of snores did wake him a time or two, though. He wondered how mercenaries on recon missions were able to sleep quietly and remain undiscovered. One of the Redwater guys snored loudly enough to scare a T-rex away, he imagined.

When the wake-up alarm chimed, the glow of day had just begun to thin the darkness. Alex rose with the vigor of a twenty-year-old, ready to dress, and explore the new land.

"Good morning everyone," Alex said to no one in particular.

Coop was already up and at the computer in the cab. "Good morning."

"Something new on the thermal cam?" Alex asked.

"No. Things are quiet. Have you noticed we haven't seen any birds?" Coop rose and arched his back.

"Yeah, I did think about that yesterday afternoon. Something's keeping the insect population in check, though. Small dinosaurs were insect eaters."

"A biological evolutionist would have a field day in this place, I bet," Coop said.

By this time Logan, Matt, and Natasha were up and getting dressed. Susan had managed to roll over. She was either too tired to pop up or perhaps waited for Coop to leave before pulling off her nightshirt.

"We're going to hit the latrine and head for breakfast," Logan said, with Natasha leading the way.

Natasha had on hiking shorts and a brown cotton shirt with the tails tied in a knot by her waist. All she needed was an Indiana Jones style hat to give her that '30s safari look. Her flip-flops flapped at a steady pace as she headed out the front cabin.

Matt looped his boot string and tightened the knot. He rose to follow after Logan.

"Matt. Hang back for a minute," Alex said.

"See you guys outside. We'll launch the drone after breakfast." Coop placed his cap on his head and left the front cabin.

Susan finally peeled herself out of the sleeping bag and dressed near a wall.

"What's up?" Matt asked, straightening his shirt collar.

"Nothing really. This trip's been at such a whirlwind pace we haven't spoken much. Are you comfortable with the mission so far? The Redwater gang, do you see anything we might need to be concerned about?"

"Not really. They are a strange bunch. Ben seems to get along with them. Hell, I don't know if he's said two words to me this entire trip. Logan told me he and Bats had come to an understanding—whatever that means. He didn't go into any detail. You know, I like Logan a lot. He's been a really good friend to me. I just . . . I just worry about him sometimes. He might be suffering from some type of depression. Not that he's moody. He's just quiet. I've tried to talk to him about it a time or two, and he's opened up a little, but he always pulls back before things get too deep. You know Logan, he can shift into the next gear in a moment's notice and turn into the life of the party," Matt said.

"Let's both keep an eye on him. In fact, we need to take responsibility for our crew and not just rely on Redwater for our protection. Not only are we as professors responsible for our students, but we're also older and better at decision-making. At some point we will be leaving the camp area and do a little exploring. I think it's best that one of our group never goes out alone with a Redwater member. At least two should stay together. In fact, either you or I need to be part of any group heading out."

"Yeah. I get it. That's a good idea. Having a figure of authority might encourage the Redwater crew to show us proper respect. Not that they haven't. But I can see them taking advantage of the others if we weren't around—especially Natasha. Those mercenaries can be an intimidating bunch."

"No doubt, though you wouldn't know it by the way Ben's acting. He's doing his damnedest to fit in with them. We need to watch and make sure he doesn't go too far. You know how things—horseplay—can get out of hand."

"Everyone is having a good time until someone gets his teeth punched out," Matt said.

"Right. If we see him going a little too far we'll rein him back."

"It's a plan."

Alex watched Susan pass and walk out of the front cabin. "Let's hit the head and eat some breakfast. This should be an exciting day."

*

"How'd you sleep?" Natasha asked while running her fingers through the long hair on the back of her head. At some point she thought she'd have to put it in a ponytail to keep cool.

"I slept okay. Couldn't stop thinking about that Protoceratops for a while. That was cool," Logan said while rubbing his hand across his chin. "I need to shave."

The two rounded the rear cabin where Coop and Suge had the drone out, preparing it for flight.

"Morning," Natasha said.

Coop grunted out a: "Morning." Both he and Suge were preoccupied and didn't bother to look up.

She turned back to Logan. "Why bother? Why don't you just let it grow? You'll look more like an explorer that way."

"Ha! I wish I could grow a beard. I may have blondish hair but hairs on my face come in black, red, and gray, too. Plus, the hair only grows in sporadic patches. I'd look ridiculous."

"How about just a moustache? Have you ever tried to grow one of them?" Natasha asked as they came upon the two latrines which were set up several yards to the opposite side of the canopy. The makeshift bathrooms consisted of a greenish tarp walled around a plastic bench with a large hole cut out on the seat. Underneath, a hole had been dug in the ground, and aromatic chemicals poured in for odor control. It was simple and it worked. Thank god there was toilet paper.

"I had a moustache before. Let's just say Burt Reynolds back in the '70s would have been a huge fan. It basically looked like a caterpillar caught up in a wind storm."

"Well, we wouldn't want that." Natasha laughed. "Me first." One of the latrines had the flap up, indicating it was occupied. She took a turn in the next one and waited for Logan. When he had finished his business, the two left for the canopy, Natasha's flip-flops snapping at each step.

Boots on ground kicked up behind her; she glanced back and saw Meat leaving the other latrine.

"Morning, Natasha. Morning, Logan," Meat said, the constant grin wide across his face.

"Morning, uh . . . Meat. Sorry, I have a hard time calling you that," Natasha said.

"Hey, Meat," Logan casually said.

"Aw, don't worry, Natasha. Everyone calls me that," Meat said, and made no attempt to catch up with the two.

"I'm sorry, but after your introduction the other night, I've forgotten your real name. I had a lot of new names to learn," Natasha kept walking.

"Clinton J. Perry, at your service. Clint's just fine by me," Meat said.

"Okay, Clint," Natasha said.

Logan turned, and said, "Eh, you don't look like a Clint. You'll always be *Meat,* to me."

Meat laughed. "Understandable."

*

As soon as Alex stepped out of the canopy he heard two taps of something hard striking another hard object, a distinct *crack,* and then sizzling and pops. He looked over and saw Ron and Caveman by the cooktop. Ron had MREs warming. Caveman hovered over a large skillet and had a spatula in his hand. "Eggs? I didn't know they brought eggs on this trip," he said to Matt.

A backpack set on the ground near Caveman, the top flipped back, with an extra-extra-extra-large, dark brown egg exposed.

"Son-of-a-bitch," Alex muttered under his breath. He cautiously approached Caveman, his mouth open in disbelief. This could not possibly be happening.

"Good morning, Prof," Caveman said. He shoved the spatula around the edges of the frying egg. "You hungry? Want some eggs? These are big. There're plenty to go around."

"Sir, I . . . Please tell me those aren't what I think they are," Alex said, trying his best to keep his cool.

"Dinosaur eggs? Yep, picked them fresh this morning," Caveman said.

By this time Natasha, Logan, and Meat had made it back to the canopy. They stopped to watch. A few others exited the canopy; either they heard the sizzling egg or came to pick up a MRE. After all, it was time for breakfast.

Alex's mouth moved as if searching for the right words. His spread arms with palms turned toward the sky pumped empty air. Then, he said, "Why?"

"'Cuz I like eggs in the morning," Caveman said, his tone couldn't have been more casual.

"But those are dinosaur eggs. Probably from that Protoceratops roaming around last night," Alex said.

"Yeah. I heard about that. Didn't see it though. I did some early morning exploring and found a nest. You ever seen eggs that big before? I have. Had a buddy that raised emus. Emu eggs are a lot prettier. They's kind of greenish blue," Caveman said.

"You had no right to take those eggs." The words had seethed out. Alex felt anger rise. His cheeks tingled.

"I didn't take them all," Caveman said, as if an excuse to absolve him from his thievery.

"But you're upsetting the balance of nature. We're interlopers here. We're a new species invading their land. We have to be careful—these creatures have found some way to survive for millions of years. We don't want to do anything to change that."

"Didn't that Darwin guy you believe in say something about the survival of the fittest?" Caveman asked.

"Yeah, but—"

"But nothing. Man's king of beasts now. And king of beasts here, too." Caveman frowned in frustration. "This thing's too big to flip. Guess I'll have to settle for scrambled eggs."

"Unbelievable!" Alex let his raised arms fall by his side.

"What's going on here?" Coop asked as he walked up.

"One of your men here took the liberty steal eggs from a dinosaur nest. He's frying one up right now in a pan. After sixty million years we find a genuine dinosaur egg, and that man over there is cooking it!" Alex released the anger.

Coop closed his eyes. His head wilted to one side. "John. What did you do?"

"Hell, Coop. I didn't do anything I don't normally do. You know how I like to live off the fat of the land," Caveman said.

"But John, you should know better. No other place on Earth is like where we are now. I thought I'd made it clear we weren't supposed to kill anything unless we didn't have a choice," Coop said.

"But I didn't kill nothing. These is just eggs," Caveman pleaded. "And I brought enough for everybody."

"That was quite thoughtful of you. But stealing the eggs was wrong. And you won't be cooking up the rest. Understand?" Coop said.

"Yeah, I got it," Caveman said.

"And you'll return those eggs as soon as you can?" Coop asked.

"Yep, I'll do that too. But I got news for you, this egg's mine, and I ain't sharing it neither," Caveman said.

Coop turned to Alex and shrugged his shoulders. "Enjoy, my friend," he told Caveman. Coop grabbed two MREs and headed back to the rear cabin.

Caveman pulled the skillet from the cooktop and stepped off to the side. He stirred the egg a bit more with the spatula, scooped some egg with it, and put a bite into his mouth. "Mmm-Mm. Them's good eggs."

*

Natasha sat next to Logan and across from Meat at the foldout table. Matt took a seat next to Alex, and he and Susan did their best to calm the man down. The rest of Redwater crew grabbed their MREs and went to the rear cabin by the drone. Ben wasn't around, so she assumed he was with them.

She had eaten her sausage patty and hash browns with bacon, and now broke off pieces of her strawberry pastry and nibbled on it. There was a plastic sleeve that came with the MREs and a small packet of salt water. She picked up the sleeve and started reading the instructions. "You use this to heat an MRE? How does that work?" she asked.

Meat wiped his mouth and finished chewing. "Inside that pouch there's a white pad—it's a heating element. What you're supposed to do is tear open the sleeve and place the unopened entrée packet inside. Then, you tear open the salt water and pour it into the sleeve. You fold the top over, and put something over it so it won't pop open—but don't seal it completely."

"So it's a chemical reaction of some sort. Does it get very hot?" Natasha asked.

"It gets hot enough to make steam. You've got to be careful that it doesn't burn you," Meat said.

"Oh, well, I'm sure that's great when you're out on a mission," Natasha said.

"I'm not complaining, but I still haven't gotten used to this powdered milk. Kind of taste like chalk," Logan said.

"Use the powdered white milk for cereal. There's chocolate powdered milk to drink," Meat said.

"Really? What's it taste like?" Logan asked.

"Chocolate flavored chalk," Meat said.

The three had a good laugh.

"Say, Natasha. I've got a question for you," Meat said.

"What is it?" She picked up the remaining half of her pastry and took a bite.

"Earlier, when we were walking back from the latrine, I saw you had a tattoo on your left heel," Meat said.

"Yes, I do," Natasha answered.

"That's some kind of Hindu God, isn't it?" Meat asked.

"It is. Shiva is an important Hindu deity. The tattoo is of Shiva as *Nataraja*—the cosmic dancer. Do you know much about Hinduism?" Natasha asks.

"No, never had a reason to," Meat said.

"I won't go too deep into it, then. Shiva is the God of destruction—a destructive force. Not an evil force. Where Brahma, another Hindu God, creates, Shiva dissolves. Shiva destroys so that Brahma may create in the rebirth. If you think about it, after the big bang, the universe is an example of creation and destruction. Stars formed from hydrogen molecules in birth, and when they go nova, they die. In doing so they created heavier elements. The process has repeated itself over billions of years. Every element in your body is recycled star material. Brahma creates, Shiva dissolves, so that the rebirth can continue," Natasha said.

"Wow, that's some deep shit." Meat pondered a moment. "You got any other tattoos?"

"No, just that one. It's not very elaborate. I guess I originally got the tattoo as a coming of age thing. After I got that one, I've had no desire for another," Natasha said.

"Yeah. Not the best artwork. I could do a much better job than that," Meat said.

"Hey, Coop's about to launch the drone," Ben called out, his head sticking through the opening of the canopy's wall.

*

Alex had regained his composure by the time he arrived by the drone. All the Redwater members were present, and he made a conscious effort to keep his gaze away from Caveman. No need to stir up anything right now. What's done is done, and hopefully such a heinous act wouldn't be repeated.

The unmanned aerial vehicle had a traditional airplane design and a wingspan about as long as an average size man. It had one engine in the middle of the back of the wing, above the rear of the fuselage. He'd seen Coop and Suge partially put it together, and surmised it was made of light material. Alex knew of various ways to launch an UAV. Some can be launched from ships and other aircraft. He'd seen hand launch and catapult launches, too. This was the first drone he'd seen with wheels.

Coop made his last few checks on the drone and walked back to the waiting crowd. "We're all set to go, Alex."

"I'm excited. Hey, how is that thing powered? Please don't tell me nuclear," Alex said, trailing off in a laugh.

"I wish. No, it's powered by a specially patented fuel cell."

"I don't see any solar panels, so I guess it doesn't use sunlight for a boost," Ben said.

"Well, fact is, the drone is made of a material that works better than a solar cell. There's not a lot of direct sunlight here, but what light that does make it gets amped up in the collector. Plus, the collector not only uses sunlight for energy, it also uses ambient heat. I figure out here we could keep it in the air for twenty-four hours before it had to have a full recharge."

"How fast will it fly?" Alex asked.

"Up to sixty miles an hour and about at five hundred feet. This bird is going to come in handy for this trip," Coop said.

"I'm ready if you are," Alex said.

Coop gave a wave to Suge, who pushed a few buttons on a laptop.

The drone's propeller buzzed into action. The wheels rolled as the UAV sped forward. In no time the front end lifted off the ground, and the modern marvel soared into the air.

All eyes followed as it flew higher over the forest and eventually out of sight.

CHAPTER 12

The laptop set strategically positioned on the table for the maximum number of viewers. Of course, Alex and Coop had front row seats. For those who didn't want to crowd around the larger screen, the drone's video stream could be watched on individual satellite phones.

Susan sat to Alex's left and fidgeted in her chair. After what seemed to be her one hundredth sigh, he resisted telling her to *Get the fuck away*. The anticipation was getting to him, too, though. It's just that she wasn't making matters any better.

The drone had been traveling at top speed for nearly two hours. Coop had the thing programed to fly around ten feet above tree level. It was boring for the most part, watching the ocean of green leaves whizzing by. He said he wanted to minimize the risk of a pterosaur mistaking the drone for something good to eat.

Alex had studied up on pterosaurs after viewing the photos released by *The International Enquirer*. Pterosaurs weren't dinosaurs. They were basically just flying lizards and the earliest vertebrate to have evolved the power of flight. The flying lizards were more closely related to birds than to any other living reptile. Pterosaurs varied in sizes, with wingspans as small as ten inches to nearly forty feet. So far, the drone had caught glimpses of pelican sized pterosaurs resting on branches during the flyby. One had raised its wings as a warning. Two bailed off the branch and flew out of the camera's range. And the other just didn't seem to give a damn.

According to the satellite map, the forest in Patagonia was thickest from where the Warthog had set camp to the largest river, which was to the west. The river was over one hundred miles away, and the expedition couldn't make it there if it wanted to. Unless, of course, they traveled on foot. Which wasn't going to happen.

The volcano was to the northwest. Another point of interest that wouldn't be visited this outing. Later today, they'd begin the journey heading southwest. And at some point, the Warthog would set permanent camp, and Coop and a few of his men would head to find the precious commodities—the true intent of this expedition.

"Looking at the radar, the drone will be arriving soon at the river," Alex said. The radar was superimposed over the satellite map, and the GPS showed the UAV as a red cross mark. The image wasn't in Google Earth detail, but was still surprisingly sophisticated. "Since we're pioneers, we have the privilege to name our discoveries after ourselves. How does the *Klasse River* sound to you?" Alex directed his joke toward Coop.

"It sounds like a trademark infringement," Coop said.

"What do you mean?"

"It's named Lear's River."

"You've already named the river?"

"Yep, and a few other major landmarks, too."

"Like the volcano?" Alex asked.

"You mean, Ace Corporation Mountain?"

Alex slowly lifted his head backward, looked at the canopy top, and shook his head. "I should have known."

"It's all about getting paid when it comes down to it," Ben said. He and the others had been surprisingly quiet.

Alex turned and saw that Natasha and Matt had peeled away and gone back in the front cabin, presumably to sit on the slightly more comfortable benches over the chairs and watch the feed on their phones. A few of the Redwater members were still there, but he didn't bother to notice who.

"Look, the treetops have disappeared. It's going over the river," Susan said, and moved to the edge of her seat.

The image showed a large clearing opening up. The mighty Lear's River cut through the dense forest like a winding snake. The drone banked to the left.

Coop's fingers danced across the keyboard. "Okay, let's slow things down a bit. I'm taking control of the drone now." The digital speedometer ticked down to 25 mph, while Coop adjusted the pitch and yaw controls using the drone's remote controller.

A grid at the bottom of the screen had Alex estimating the river was around 40 yards wide at this point. There were no whitecaps in the water, so he doubted the current was very strong. The drone rolled slightly to follow the path, and once past a few tall trees by the water, one of time's most incredible scenes imaginable unfolded before them.

"Oh my God . . ." Susan said barely above a whisper.

"Look!" Matt cried out from the front cabin.

The computer screen showed the river gently rolling past an incredibly massive sauropod wading by the bank. It was brownish and lime green in color, with long vertical stripes on a portion of its side. The front two legs were noticeably longer than the rear. Its tail protruded above the water as it moved its small head swiveling on a long neck to reach the leaves of a nearby tree.

"This makes the movie *Jurassic Park* look homemade," Alex said. "I didn't realize the camera was of such high resolution. Look at the details of those markings on his body."

"When we pass, I'll zoom in on the head," Coop said.

The beast turned to look at the interloper, chewing on the last mouthful of leaves. The eyes were relatively small above a wide muzzle and thick jawbones. An arch of bone rose over the snout and in front of the eyes, encircling the nasal opening.

"Look at those teeth. They look like fat carrots," Ben said.

Matt and Natasha stepped out of the front cabin. Logan let Natasha stand in front of him. He watched the screen over her head, while Matt stood behind him and looked over his shoulder.

"That's a mighty big hoss right there," Caveman said.

"I think it's a Brachiosaurus," Alex said.

"Barack-E-O-saurus? They named a dinosaur after the president?"

Suge and a few others chuckled. Alex wasn't sure if Caveman had floated a joke or if he was just demonstrating his acumen. Right now, he really didn't care to find out.

"Those things can get over eighty feet long and weigh over forty tons. I did read that the neck can lift the head to around thirty feet," Alex said. "They aren't meat eaters, but I wouldn't want to get too close to one."

"You know what that stuff is between Brontosaurus toes?" Caveman asked. No one took the bait. So after a few moments, he delivered the punchline, "Slow natives."

A comedian the man was not.

"Are you going to circle and get more video?" Alex asked.

"No, I want to keep going. I—look, there's more," Coop said.

More sauropods appeared in the distance, on the opposite side of the river. Three hulking beasts zoomed into view as the drone approached. One was the same color as the first Brachiosaurus. The other two were shaped a bit differently. The front legs were the same length as the back legs. Same long neck and small head, but the tails were noticeably longer.

When Alex thought about it, the Brachiosaurus' basic build looked similar to a giraffe's. The body angled upward from the tail, and the long neck gave it a more upright appearance.

The other two sauropods, which were elephant gray in color, had a more elongated look. The tail was as long as the neck.

"Those could be a species of sauropod called *Diplodocus*. I'm not educated enough to differentiate between the various species of sauropods," Alex said.

"Man, look at that. Lumbering along, cooling their heels at the beach, not a care in the world. No boats passing by. No people whooping and hollering. No sky-rises in the distance. No garbage. No pollution. No humans to fuck things up. Makes you think that the world was meant to be this way. Makes you wonder if mankind was just one big mistake. Mother Nature's finest creation might end up being the death of her," Ben said, the insightful comment was a bit out of place from his usually whimsical demeanor.

"But man is here now," Natasha said.

"Yes, and we need to make damned sure we don't fuck things up," Alex said, not turning from the screen.

"What's that? Is that a Tyrannosaurus?" Susan said, and poked the air toward the screen.

The drone banked to the right and leveled out as a large theropod dipped his head at the river's edge. It certainly looked like a T-rex.

"It just might be. If it is, I don't think it's mature. There are other theropods that might look similar. But if that guy was full grown there'd be no doubt about it. Wait until we get a better look at the head," Alex said.

The dinosaur raised its head from the water after taking a drink and stood upright, its short arms tucked against its chest. The drone was close enough to show the brownish-skinned creature also sported small feathers at the crown of its head. The feathers ran the length of the spine and became larger at the tip of the tail. This species was of a rather plain looking variety. One thing for sure, the massive jaws and rows of sharp teeth made it look anything but friendly.

"It could be an Allosaurus. A grown Allosaurus is only around seventy-five percent the size of a grown T-rex. We don't know the age of this one. There're other theropods that are larger than T-rex. There's a Giganotosaurus, a Spinosaurus, and another one I can't remember the name of that grow larger," Alex said.

"Yeah, but the Spinosaurus had a large sail like flap of skin on the back, so it's not that," Matt added. "This one's alone. I read somewhere that some theropods hunted in packs."

"That's a scary thought, a pack of these things chasing after you," Logan said.

The drone flew past and continued its journey down the river.

"I wonder what we'll see next," Susan said. Her right cheek pressed on Alex's left arm as she craned her head for a better view of the computer screen.

"The river's widening," Coop said, and shifted the weight of his buttocks on the seat.

Both sides of the river opened into a large expanse, and then narrowed back down in the distance, creating a circular shaped lake of sorts. From the looks of things, this was one popular watering hole; prehistoric creatures abounded.

"Would you look at that," Alex marveled.

Clumps of dinosaurs surround the water's edge on both sides, some in small herds. One larger herd contained Triceratops. What would a group of Triceratops be called? Alex had no clue. This bunch had dinosaurs of two distinct colors. One variety was a dull brown, and the other a light green—sort of the same color as a grass snake. Knowing nature, Alex figured the green, more eye-appealing variety were males. Nature had a way of giving beauty to the male species in animals. That certainly wasn't true of humans. But the way society was headed today, some males worked hard in changing the course of evolution.

"I'm going put the drone back in autopilot. I'm going to have it circle this area so we can get a long look at this," Coop said.

"That's going to make me dizzy watching that," Ben said, and took a step back and rubbed his eyes.

"I'll put the camera in three-sixty mode. We'll be able to set a point on the computer for the camera to focus on," Coop said.

"Oh, great," Ben said.

"Right there. Click on the Stegosauruses," Alex said.

The camera fixed on seven or eight of the strange, colorful creatures. Markings on their bodies reminded Alex of those of a reticulated Gila monster lizard. The orange and black pattern covered their bodies, but the black turned into bands near the spiked tails. Spade like armor plates, reddish in color, ran the length from the head to the tail, increasing in size along the back.

"Those things are magnificent." Alex let the sight set in for several long moments. "Okay, pan around."

Different sized theropods, none nearly as big as the T-rex they saw earlier, though, wandered about alone or in small groups. Alex figured some of the smaller ones were of the insect eating variety. Insects would take over anywhere without natural predators.

"What's that one right there? It has shorter front legs like a theropod, but it walks on four legs like a sauropod," Ben said.

"Oh, God, let me think . . . might be an *Edmontosaurus*—see the duckbill? But those things can get huge. Might be a young one . . . there's a few more over there." Alex felt like a kid in a candy store; he wanted to stop and eat, but didn't want to overlook a tasty new treat. "Oh, wait. Stop there . . . those theropods . . . I think those are Velociraptors."

"But those have feathers and look smaller than the ones in *Jurassic Park*," Ben said.

"Yeah, that's how I know they're Velociraptors."

"Okay, got it," Ben said, as if he wished he could have taken his ignorant comment back.

"There's one, two, three, four, five of them," Alex counted.

"They're all huddled up. What are they doing?" Natasha asked.

"Looks like they might be hunting something. Coop, pan over to the left a bit," Alex said.

The camera moved over; three Triceratops had drifted away from the herd, two adults, one male and one female, and the other a young calf. The younger one was light brown in color. Alex assumed it was a female too.

The Velociraptors hid in wait for attack. Nature had a dark side, and those that survived depended on those who would have to die.

The male led the way, with the female close by, and the calf waddling behind. The rest of the herd meandered in tow.

The Velociraptors sunk low near the ground in wait of the ambush. Alex almost cried out a warning, and realized the total futility of such action. Two of the Velociraptors' tails began to twitch; they were the first to spring out and attack.

The Triceratops bull abruptly came to a halt as distance quickly closed between him and the predators. In no time, he spun around and ran faster than Alex thought possible back toward the herd, passing the cow, and the calf, too. The whole herd caught wind of the ordeal. The exodus was on.

The cow ran past her calf, which saw the coming danger. Awkwardly, the calf turned near the edge of the bank and tumbled down to the river a few feet away.

All five Velociraptors dove over the edge. The first two attacked the calf in the water, one sinking its chops into one side of her frill, the armor crown that rose from the head. The other lowered itself near the water. Its teeth searching for the soft spot of the neck. Another chomped down on the back, trying to keep movement at minimum. The poor little thing opened her beak-like mouth, in what Alex could only imagine was a tearful cry for mercy. The small horn on the tip of her nose and the two bull-like horns above her eyes were too small of a deterrent for the ferocious Velociraptors.

"The poor thing! It's going to die!" Susan screeched and dug her nails into Alex's left arm.

Cries of exasperation burst from behind.

"Oh no," Natasha wailed. She turned and clung on to Matt.

Alex turned at her cry and caught a brief glimpse of his love holding onto another man. His anger kicked up a notch, as if Susan already didn't have him in a pissy mood, and he turned back to watch the slaughter.

The Triceratops calf clung to life, her legs submerged under water, but fighting for all she was worth. Another Velociraptor bit onto the frill, and the group worked to move the calf toward dry land. The fifth Velociraptor raised its body up. Its head snaked back and forth—as if watching something in the distance.

"What's that in the water?" Susan said.

Something long and large slowly floated toward the fray.

"It looks like a log," Ben said.

"That ain't no log," Caveman said.

About that time, the *log* opened its mouth and attacked the Velociraptor by the water's edge.

"It's a crocodile!" Ben yelled.

The Velociraptor jumped backward as two rows of teeth chomped the air between them. The raptor didn't flee and was determined to stand its ground. It snapped and bit the croc on the long tapered snout. The croc thrashed its thick tail about and jerked itself free.

The croc wasn't giving up now. The Triceratops' tail was right there for the taking. The croc bit down and tried to steal the prize.

"No!" Natasha squealed.

The tug of war was on. Four Velociraptors pulled on up the bank while the crocodile pulled toward the water. The struggle continued for over a minute.

"I can't believe this. How is that Triceratops still alive?" Ben said.

With great effort, the Velociraptors inched the calf away from the water until they had her on land. Amazingly, she still stood on her own accord—refusing to fall and be gutted by the predators.

The croc had its front feet on the bank when the fifth raptor bit down on its neck. The croc let go of the Triceratops' tail, and with a violent shake of its body—pulled free of the raptor—and sought refuge in the river.

The Velociraptors surrounded the Triceratops; their teeth sunk into her body, patiently waiting for her to fall.

"That's a tough little sumbitch, there," Caveman said.

Alex couldn't help but agree. Still, it would be only a matter of seconds before a fatal bite would take down the relativity small dinosaur.

Suddenly, the Velociraptor on watch took a step or two back and rose up in defiance.

"Something's up. Can you zoom out a bit?" Alex asked.

The camera pulled back, and the lead Triceratops had grown a set and returned for his calf.

"Look at that! Poppa bull says he wants a piece of that ass," Caveman said.

But it wasn't just *Poppa bull*, the rest of the herd followed close behind him. A Triceratops is more than six times the size of a Velociraptor. Even though they were slower and didn't have the assault capabilities of the theropods, they were a massive force to deal with. Poppa bull edged his way in, and with head low to the ground, jutted forward—leading with his horned beak and two horns of his head, forcing the Velociraptor to flee down the bank a ways. The raptor stopped and turned back toward the bull, who then charged with horns lowered—sending the theropod scampering away for good.

"Damn! I can't believe that raptor pussed out like that," Ben said.

"The Triceratops' head is like armor," Alex said.

The other Velociraptors continued the death hold, unwilling to let go of their victim, which by all accounts, from what Alex saw, was the stupidest thing possible. If they killed the calf they'd never get a chance to eat it. The herd of Triceratops could stampede them to death in an instant.

The bull returned to the herd, which had a few of the other braver bulls edging up to the Velociraptors piled around the calf. Not all of the Triceratops had what it took to stay in the fight, despite the size advantage. Some would instantly retreat when a raptor snapped to stand its ground.

After tasting victory, Poppa bull must have felt invincible. He charged one of the raptors—his horn jabbing it in the side. With a quick thrust of his head, the Velociraptor sailed through the air and landed flat on the ground. It immediately rose and fled like a scalded dog.

Cheers erupted from behind Alex. This would be a fight of historical proportions.

And then there were three. The theropods held their prey but remained as low to the ground as possible.

The herd inched its way toward them—an impenetrable wall of mass and armor.

The raptors let go of the calf. It trotted on shaky legs into the herd.

More cheers and thanks rose from the expedition members.

"This is about to get good," Caveman said.

With the Velociraptors clearly outnumbered, they at least had enough sense *to get while the getting was good.* One leaped up and ran down the river's bank as fast as its two legs would carry it.

The other two remained low, and when a female Triceratops attacked from the side, the other two decided it was time to leave, too.

"I can't believe, after all that, that the calf lived," Susan said.

"That was simply amazing," Alex said, feeling physically and emotionally drained after the ordeal.

The image on the computer screen abruptly shifted from the ground, past the trees, and then turned up into blue sky. The imagine darkened for a few seconds and then turned to blue sky again.

"What happened?" Alex asked.

"Not good," Coop said. "Not good at all." He tried to maneuver the drone with zero successes. The computer screen went blank.

"Th-th-th-tha-tha-tha-that's all, folks!" Caveman said, imitating his beloved Porky Pig.

"Something got the drone," Alex said.

"I'm afraid so. Probably a pterosaur. I was afraid something like this might happen," Coop said.

"I'm sure we don't have another, right?" Alex said.

"No, show's over, folks," Coop said.

Alex slapped the table in frustration, and then brought his hands up to his temples. He let out a deep breath, and asked, "Okay, so what's the plan now?"

Coop put the remote control on the table and closed the laptop. "Time to pack up. Wagon's heading southwest."

CHAPTER 13

The drone had been the window to this savage world, but in reality, Alex knew they were smack dab in it—just at the edge. There wasn't much left to the imagination now as to what dangers lurked beyond. Getting up front and personal with the indigenous wildlife wasn't the best of ideas. Still, it was a shame that contact would be limited to creatures that happened to wander across their path.

It took a little more than an hour to put away the canopy, pack up the rear cabin, and fill in the latrine holes. The most evidence that man had come through were slight imprints on the ground from the Warthog's and Mule's treads.

The caravan kept to its previous schedule, rolling along as fast as the terrain would allow, and taking rest stops every couple of hours. Alex was unsure of how much actual distance they traveled. The path shifted from open plains, to rocky hills, to sparsely populated forests. The pristine beauty of the hidden land held Alex in awe.

Dinosaurs of the less threatening variety roamed freely and none seemed to be curious enough to approach the mechanized vehicles traveling across their land. The expedition spooked a herd of Gallimimus when the vehicles happened upon it. The dinosaurs were ostrich-like, with small heads, toothless beaks, large eyes, long necks, short arms, long legs, and long tails. Alex chuckled when he read that *Gallimimus* meant 'chicken mimic,' which was a great description of how the dinosaur ran. The Gallimimuses didn't have feathers and were rather plain in their tan colored skin. Caveman had wondered aloud how tasty a fried leg might be.

There was a noticeable absence of large carnivores, which didn't upset anyone. But there seemed to be a good supply of food across the land traveled thus far, so that he thought they'd have come across a giant theropod by now.

Coop had said water was plentiful on the land. Lear's River, though, was by far the biggest waterway. Perhaps most of the larger dinosaur life resided in that area. The drone didn't have a chance to do much exploring before meeting its untimely demise. There was so much to learn, and now one their greatest tools had been taken from them.

Alex and others took turns looking out the overhead hatch. The wind felt warm against his cheeks and ruffled his hair. There were times the Warthog neared 60 mph. The sulphur odor in the air diminished the farther south they traveled. Occasionally, he'd get a whiff of something organic rotting. It reminded him of being at the zoo.

Ben had pestered Ron to the point that the big man let him take the Warthog's wheel. From what Alex could tell, it drove like any standard vehicle. Gas pedal, brake, steering wheel, all set on the right hand side. No doubt as to its European origin.

Ron didn't seem to mind giving up his seat. In fact, he enjoyed Ben's interest, giving him pointers on how soon to start turning, and when to speed up and slow down when avoiding obstacles. Of all the college group, Ben was the most accepted by the Redwater gang. Alex didn't know what was behind Ben's involvement with the mercenary group. Was he trying to prove something to them? Was he trying to prove something to himself? Perhaps he admired the former soldiers of war.

Maybe in his mind Ben thought of them as *real* men. Men that risked life, limb—everything. Soldiers were far superior to athletes. Investing their blood, sweat, and tears to preserve freedom. Freedom for the athletes to sculpt their bodies, ingest expensive dietary supplements, and earn huge amounts of money for performing on a stage. Alex didn't know if that was the case for Ben, but for him, he knew it to be so.

"Whoa . . . we got a visitor up ahead," Ben called out from the cab.

About that time, Matt, who had been looking out the hatch, patted the inside of the roof with his hand. He spoke, but Alex couldn't make out the words.

Alex had been hanging around the cab entrance, watching through a small portion of the windshield. His mind had wandered off but immediately snapped-to when Ben gave his warning.

The Mule and Warthog slowed to a stop. Everyone stood and waited for a report.

"There's a T-rex about twenty yards away," Ben said.

"What's he doing?" Chief asked.

"Looks like he's having lunch," Ben said.

Coop pushed his way up to Alex, who quickly stepped out of the man's way. "Excuse me." Coop waited for Ron to move and then sat in the co-pilot seat. "I'll fire up one of the cameras and stream the video too if you want to watch on your phones."

Coop's laptop screen woke from its sleep. The camera panned until it stopped on the T-rex. The image zoomed in on the thunder lizard.

"Wow, that thing is huge," Natasha said from somewhere inside the crowd.

Chief walked over by Matt and tapped him on the leg. "Hey, you need to come on down. I need to man the gun in case there's any trouble."

"You aren't going to shoot it, are you?" Susan asked.

"Not if I don't have to," Chief said, and moved out of Matt's way as he stepped down the ladder. He immediately climbed up onto the Warthog's roof.

The T-rex hadn't taken notice of the expedition, and seemed content eating the Gallimimus unfortunate enough to cross his path.

"Looking at the grid, this guy is nearly thirty feet long," Coop said, and then zoomed in closer.

"Look at its skin. What's wrong with it?" Ben asked.

This T-rex was from a gray variety and had short stripe markings down its spine. It, too, had feathers of some sort at the end of its tail. But what had caught Ben's eye was the poor condition of the mighty beast.

"I don't know. Maybe it's been in a few fights in its lifetime," Alex said.

"Yeah, looks like it lost a couple," Ben said.

"Wait, is something wrong with its ears? Can you get a closer shot of the head?" Matt asked.

Coop zoomed in on the side of the head as the dinosaur lowered for another mouthful.

"Its ears. They look deformed—grown over," Matt said.

"Yeah. The other T-rex's ears we saw didn't look like that," Natasha said.

"Because of the size and its overall condition, I'd say that this is one old dinosaur. Maybe that's why it's here—apart from other large dinosaurs. Maybe it's too old to defend itself from younger, healthier ones. In fact, I don't know if due to age or his ear deformity, if it can hear. It hasn't sensed us yet. You saw how all the other dinosaurs reacted when our vehicles drove by," Alex said.

"Yeah, but this is a T-rex. He ain't afraid of nothing," Caveman said.

"He may not be afraid, but he's given no evidence that he knows we're here. I say we just ease on down the road and see what happens," Coop said. He pushed the radio mic on the dash. "Chief, you ready in case it gets too close?"

"Roger. I've got a few rounds of non-lethal explosives ready to go if I need them. I will follow up with the heavy stuff if necessary," Chief said.

"I trust your judgement," Coop said.

"Heading out," Don called from the Mule's radio.

"Roger," Coop said.

The Mule traveled a good twenty yards before Coop gave Ben the okay to follow. The T-rex never once looked in their direction and steadily pulled meat from bone with its sharp teeth and massive jaws.

"Well, that was a whole lot of nothing," Caveman said.

"Yeah, well, when you get too old to hear you'll be just like him," Suge said. "Your head in a bowl, gumming you grits in the old folks home."

"Not me, partner. I ain't ever gonna let myself get in that condition. I've found a cure for old age," Caveman said.

"Ha. Bullshit," Suge said. "You're probably going to get so fat you won't be able to wipe your ass. How are you going to cure that?"

"Easy, it's called three fifty-seven magnum," Caveman said.

Suge started to speak, then stopped himself, and shrugged his shoulders. "Can't argue with that."

The two vehicles hit high gear not long after passing the ageing dinosaur, heading southwest.

The T-rex sniffed around the Gallimimus' carcass and didn't find anything left it cared to eat. It slowly raised its body as upright as it could. Its tired eyes looked about as if searching for more food. Its gaze finally fixed upon an area of land where brush had been flattened. The dinosaur put its nose in the air, and underneath blood stained teeth, snaked its gray and pitted tongue about. With uncertainty, it turned its massive body and raised a clawed foot toward the disturbance, each step cautious until arriving at the strange footprints marking its land, the territory it alone ruled.

The dinosaur let out a cry into the humid jungle air. It put its head down, and with determined steps, followed the beast daring to invade its land.

*

By the time the Warthog entered an area too overgrown with trees to continue, the sun had shared its last bit of light. It was time again to set up camp.

"All right, folks. This is going to be home base for the remainder of the trip," Coop said as he left the cab and entered the front cabin.

"So soon? For some reason I was under the impression we had another day's travel," Alex said, raising his arms back in a stretch.

"After seeing the potential dangers at Lear's River, I picked an alternate site. The original plan was to bring you farther south and on a less direct route—to accommodate for the Warthog's size. Lear's River winds its way too close to where you would have set camp. The river seems to be a haven for dinosaurs. I wouldn't want to put you too close to that," Coop said.

"No, I guess not," Alex said.

"Anyway, I'm closer to my destination. And the Mule won't have any problems navigating the terrain," Coop said. "There is a creek about a half mile to the west. You have to get your water from there. Just follow Chief's orders, and don't stray too far from the Warthog. I trust my men will keep you safe."

"Okay, same routine as before. Don will set up the perimeter lights. Let's get the canopy pulled out and the sides up, and get the latrines going before chow time," Chief said. He stepped over to the front cabin's door and slowly opened it. "Don't forget the insect repellant."

*

Something Alex ate had kept him up a good portion of the night. He wasn't sure if it was the Thai Chicken MRE or the cheese spread with Jalapenos packaged with it. Everything tasted fine while he ate it, but not long after, he started burping, followed by expelling odorous flatulence. If this was a *men's only* trip, he'd make Caveman pay for gassing them the other day.

As it was, he'd spent as much time in the latrine as he did his sleeping bag up until 4 a.m. Thankfully, he fell fast asleep afterward.

When Alex awoke he was the only one still inside the front cabin. The other sleeping bags were rolled up and stored by the wall. He slowly rose on one arm and wiped the crust from his eyes. A foul taste remained in his dry mouth, and his rear was irritated from wiping with paper towels. What had happened to the toilet paper they had used earlier? *First World Problems*, for sure.

Alex craned his neck to the side and saw the canopy area was also vacant. What time was it? After a deep breath, he rolled out of bed and put the sleeping bag away. It was time to dress and face the wonders of a new day, hopefully not from inside a latrine.

When he stepped out from canopy's doorway, Bats and Suge had supplies in their arms, walking from the rear cabin, and heading toward the Mule.

"Feeling better, Professor?" Suge asked.

"Uh, yeah. I think so. Are you guys getting ready to leave?" Alex asked.

"Heading out in fifteen," Suge said as he and Bats walked past.

It was 8:30 a.m. The sun had been up for only an hour. Alex gazed about and found evidence that breakfast had come and gone. No matter. He wasn't in the mood for anything other than a cold bottle of water.

Coop and Don came from the rear cabin, their rifles over their shoulders.

"Morning, Professor. Rough night?" Coop said.

"Yeah. Those paper towels made it even rougher," Alex said.

Coop chuckled. "Sorry, we only had a few rolls of two-ply."

"I'll heal. Say, where is everyone else?"

"Oh, they're on the other side of the rear cabin. Caveman's made some friends," Coop said. "Go check it out." Coop and Don moved on.

Alex stepped over to the rear cabin's open door and saw the remainder of the crew piled up behind Caveman, about twenty yards away. He took out a bottle of water from the cooler, twisted off the cap, and chugged a mouthful.

Caveman stooped and had his arm extended. From some light brush nearby, a tiny theropod, brownish in color, cautiously stepped into view.

Alex took another drink and headed toward the crew. The mercenary had made a friend, all right. And he was feeding it like it was a squirrel in a public park.

"That's right, little one. Take the cracker," Caveman said as if he spoke to a toddler.

"Why is this man feeding that dinosaur?" Alex said as he reached the group.

Matt turned, and said, "He's been out here since sunup. I told him he shouldn't be feeding the wildlife, but he didn't listen to me."

"I wonder if we can teach that thing tricks," Ron said.

"I doubt it. But if it decides it likes the taste of human flesh, we might have a problem on our hands," Alex said, hoping to spread a little fear.

Natasha was off to the side. She had her camera and steadily took pictures.

"What is it?" Ron asked.

"It's a Compsognathus," Alex said.

"How big do they get?"

"About the size of a chicken or a turkey, it depends on the species. That one's only about twelve inches tall. It should grow some more. Unless it chokes on the cracker."

The Compsognathus stopped less than a foot away from Caveman's hand, stretched out its neck, and bit down on the cracker. It leaned back and brought its small three digit hands up to the treat. After tasting a piece, it let the cracker fall to the ground, and turned and scurried back into the brush.

Caveman straightened up, turned, and frowned.

"A Compsognathus is a meat eater. You're lucky it didn't go for your finger," Alex said.

"Ah, that little thing couldn't do me no harm. Heck, when I was a kid, we used to catch them green lizards and let them bite our earlobes—let 'em hang like earrings," Caveman said.

"Yes, but you might find these *lizards* have real teeth capable of tearing flesh. Not only that, you need to worry about the bacteria in their mouths. The bacteria could be so deadly that it might act like a poison and kill you," Alex said, inching up the fear factor.

"You might want to listen to what the professor says, John," Coop said. He and his three companions walked up. "The man is an expert in zoology. You might learn a thing or two from him. His advice might even save your life one day."

Caveman adjusted his cap and lowered his head, keeping his thoughts to himself.

"You guys about to head out?" Chief asked, and he approached Coop.

"Yep. The Mule's loaded with everything we need. Shouldn't be gone much longer than a week. We'll keep you updated at the designated check-in times," Coop said. He turned his attention to Alex. "Everything good?"

"I believe so. We'll take things slow and avoid making stupid mistakes. Chief will be calling the shots. We're in good hands," Alex said.

"Good to hear," Coop said.

"Roll tide," Don said to Ron.

"Roll tide," Ron replied.

Suge gave a quick salute and turned. Bats gave a brief nod goodbye before following. The four men headed for the Mule.

Chief faced his audience. "Listen up, everyone. I've looked at the basic map and decided, for now, to limit our excursions to no more than a half mile from the Warthog. We'll keep to that for the next few days or until we decided it's safe and worth the risk to venture farther. Today we'll play it conservative. We've used a good amount of water so far on the trip, and Coop and his bunch took their share. There's a creek within that half-mile distance to the west. One group will leave now and bring water back to the purifier. After lunch, the other group will go.

"You can use this time to combine work and pleasure. Bring your cameras and take your time learning the lay of the land. The creek is only a fifteen-minute walk away, so take a couple of hours. Just be back before lunch.

"Meat," Chief singled the big man out, "you and Caveman are in charge of the first group. There're four water backpacks in the rear cabin capable of holding fifteen gallons of water each. That's over a hundred pounds, people. So don't put more water in than you are able to carry.

"Ron and I will go out with the next group. So, who's going first?" Chief asked.

"I'd be better off going with the next group," Alex said. "Matt, you're in charge of this one."

"Okay." Matt thought a moment. "I'll take Logan and Natasha with me."

Well, that wasn't much of a surprise. Logan and Matt had become pretty good buddies in the last few months. And there was no way Matt wasn't going to pass up an opportunity to spend more time with Natasha.

Alex gave Matt a thumb-up approval, and the first group headed to the rear cabin to get their gear for the hike.

"What are we going to do?" Susan asked Alex.

"Well, I guess we can grab some binoculars and get on top of the Warthog, take a look around. We ought to spend some time cataloguing some of the plants, too."

Ben stepped up. "I'll get our guns and make sure they're ready to go." He turned to Ron. "Hey, you going to give me one of those rifles?"

Ron turned to Chief, who rolled his eyes. Ron said, "Tell you what, I'll let you wrestle Caveman for his."

Ben deflated. "The day he loses two arms and a leg, I'll think about it."

*

Natasha donned a water backpack, and clipped her gun and canteen on her belt. Her satellite phone was fully charged, and her digital SLR camera hung around her neck.

Logan pushed his arms through the water backpack's straps and cinched it up. He watched Meat approach Natasha.

The mercenary had a backpack of his own and carried his rifle. Something in the way he looked at Natasha told Logan the man had something on his mind.

"Uh, hey, Natasha," Meat said. He held his JNY-7 in his right hand and had his left arm pulled against his chest.

"Hey, Clint," Natasha said. "Ready to go?"

"Sure," he said, hovering over, wearing a wide, shy smile. "I wanted to show you something."

She narrowed her eyes and turned her head slightly to the side. "Is it alive?"

"Nah . . . Here, look at my new tattoo." The Samoan presented his left forearm for her to see.

Logan stepped closer to get a look. The tattoo looked like the exact picture of Natasha with a rose in her hair that Meat had drawn the day they arrived in Patagonia. His skin was a bit red around the tattoo's edge, but the image itself was one of the clearest and most detailed he'd ever seen.

"It's . . . It's me. Wow. Clint, what made you do that? Why'd you put me on your arm?" Natasha asked, surprised, but sounding more honored than creeped out.

Logan was creeped out.

"The other day after our talk about Shiva destroying so that Brahma can create, and how you told me our bodies are made up of dead stars, it . . . it gave me a new way to think about life. That meant something to me. So, I wanted to have a picture of you with me at all times—for inspiration. To remind me that the basics of life are wondrous and how I need to look beyond only what my eyes can see," Meat said.

"I'm so glad we had the talk, then. And, I'm honored by your tattoo," Natasha said.

"You folks about ready?" Caveman walked up behind Logan.

"Y'all go ahead. I'll catch up." Matt had his canteen out and was in the process of filling it. He still needed to don his backpack.

"Come on," Caveman said. "I'm ready to see some more of them critters."

Logan didn't feel good about leaving without Matt, and thought it seemed like Matt was purposely delaying departure. Then he saw Matt remove a small tube of toothpaste from his pocket, put some on his finger, and rub it across his teeth. Natasha certainly wasn't without her admirers this trip.

Logan shook his head and followed after Meat and Natasha.

"Hey," Caveman said as he walked by Logan's side. "You heard what they called the first gay dinosaur?"

Okay, here we go. Was this cretin trying to get under his skin or was he in his own way trying to make friends? "No, I don't know what they called the first gay dinosaur. But I'm afraid I'm about to."

"Ha, well, the first gay dinosaur . . . they called it, the Mega-sore-ass." Caveman barely finished the sentence before breaking out in laughter. "Get it? Sore-ass."

"Oh yes, I got it," Logan said, thinking the joke would be popular with preteens.

"How about the first lesbian dinosaur?" Caveman asked.

"Uh, do we have—"

"It was called the Lick-a-lota-puss." Caveman giggled uncontrollably and turned a slight shade of pink.

Logan didn't really find the jokes offensive and didn't think Caveman had any malicious intent behind them. The mercenary's laughter was particularly infectious. Logan started giggling, too.

CHAPTER 14

"So then, we're about halfway to the creek according to the GPS, when I hear something rustling the grass." Matt downed a slug of water and wiped his mouth with the back of his hand. "I freeze and motion for Caveman, who was bringing up the rear, to be ready."

Open MRE bags littered the table. Most everyone had finished eating. Matt, though, still had half his entrée left. He had been too excited to finish his food before recounting the morning's adventure.

"I made sure Natasha was behind me. You know, in case we were attacked. I had my pistol out, so did Logan, and Natasha was ready to shoot whatever it was with her camera. Finally, this thing comes from around a clump of trees so we can see it. At first, I thought it was a pig," Matt said.

"If it were a pig we'd be eating ham sandwiches for lunch," Caveman said.

Alex closed his eyes and shook his head. Matt realized the professor was doing his best to keep the peace and ignore the mercenary.

Caveman must have noticed Alex's reaction, because he said, "What? I ain't supposed to kill dinosaurs. Nobody said nothing about killing an ordinary pig."

Alex grabbed his MRE bag and crumpled it in his hand. He must have felt the bag wasn't empty and opened it back up. A small packet of food had remained, and whatever it was, Alex thought it valuable enough to save for later. He put the packet in his front pocket.

"Yeah, well, I don't think we'll be seeing any pigs on this trip. Anyway, this thing is the size of a small pig—around three feet. It's eating plants and doesn't seem to know we're around. It's gray in color, and in reality, it looked more like a hippo than a pig." Matt jabbed a meatball with his spork, brought it to his mouth, and bit half of it off. He chewed quickly, and continued, "Natasha shot a few pictures before it caught wind of us and trotted off. I looked it up on my satellite phone. It's called a *Phosphatherium*. Turns out, it's an ancestor of the elephant, not hippos or pigs."

"Elephant, the other white meat…" Caveman said. The pun hung in the air without comment.

"That was a cool thing to see." Matt finished the other half of the meatball. "There was more. A lot more. Not everything would get close enough to give us a good look."

"Yeah, there were tons of pterosaurs hiding in the trees. It was hard to notice them at first," Logan said. "The smaller ones migrate to the lower branches. I saw one eating insects, and it was just a little larger than my hand."

"I read all pterosaurs eat insects, in the early stages of life. The larger ones move up to small reptiles and fish. They'll even eat carrion," Alex said.

"The small pterosaur looked like a toy," Logan continued. "They varied in shapes, sizes, and colors—nothing exotic, mind you. We didn't see anything larger than an emu, which was scary large enough. I think humans might be too big of a threat for the ones we encountered."

"Right before we got to the creek, I heard something really large in the woods," Natasha said. "Clint had his rifle ready when the thing lumbered into view. It must have been eight feet long and around three feet high. It reminded me of a cross between a toad and a lizard. I don't think it was very smart. Its skin looked thick, like some type of armor. It passed a few feet from us and never bothered to even look our way."

"I looked it up later and found out it's an Ankylosaur—but get this. This species is called a minmi," Matt said.

"Mini-Me?" Ben said. He raised his eyebrows and pursed his lips, slowly bringing his little finger up to the bottom of his mouth. "Did Doctor *E-vil* offer you . . . one *million* dollars for the Mini-me?"

"Not Mini-Me, goofball. Minmi. Named after a location where its fossils were found," Matt said, thinking it had been a while since Ben had acted his usual clown self with the crew. Ben had been spending more time with the Redwater men. Now that his audience was cut in half, he had to go back to his old ways to get attention.

"What about the creek?" Susan asked.

"The creek is beautiful. It's only about twenty feet wide and has the clearest water I've ever seen. The bank is rocky, and you can walk on rocks into the creek a little ways. I doubt the deepest part is over your head. Not sure of the temperature, but it was warm to the touch. Even if it's a spring feed creek the magma is so close to the Earth's surface it'd warm it up," Matt said.

"Did you see much wildlife? Any fish?" Susan asked.

"Saw several small theropods by the water's edge when we got there. They scattered. There were minnow sized fish in the area, so I guess they were fishing. On the other side of the bank, a Protoceratops and family came down for a drink. But I guess the most unique creature we saw was this four footed mammal that reminded me a lot of a medium sized dog. It had fur, and its face was longer than a canine's. Get this, it's called a *Pakicetus*, and it's the ancestor to modern whales," Matt said.

"*Bullshit*," Caveman voiced in a mock sneeze. "There ain't no way I'm ever gonna believe that something the size of a dog lived on land and growed flippers and swole up to the size of an eighteen wheeler. What proof is there for scientists to think that?"

"I read that the inner ear of the Pakicetus is similar to that of whales. Beyond that, I don't know," Matt said.

"That's all they got? The inner ear? I might have been born at night, but I wasn't born last night." Caveman rose from his chair, and said, "Shit's getting deep in here," and then stormed off.

"I don't know about the shit getting deep, but I'm tired of hearing about all the stuff you saw. I'm ready to head out and see some stuff for myself," Ben said.

"All right then, Ron and I'll get our guns and—" Chief started.

"I've got the water backpacks and most of our stuff right over there—ready to go." Ben popped up from his seat and headed to the pile of equipment off to the side.

"I'll get our cameras and hats," Alex said and rose from the table, and then headed into the front cabin.

He returned a couple of minutes later with his hands full. He went over and gave Susan her things, and said, "I'm going to fill up the canteen." Alex turned and left.

The day was bright, but the perpetual vapor cloud overhead played tricks with the lighting at times. It reminded Alex of the wintertime when the Earth shifted on its axis—deflecting the sun's rays. He could see just fine, but it was as if his eyes hungered for a bit more light.

Another day would come and go, and another day he would miss Natasha's sweet embrace. A time or two at lunch he felt a compulsion just to stand, pull Natasha up by the hand, and take her in his arms in front of everyone—right in the middle of Matt droning on and on about what they saw earlier. He tried to imagine the surprised expression on the associate professor's face had he done that. Susan's reaction, too, for that matter. Fuck Matt. Fuck Susan. Fuck Caveman and everyone else on this goddamned trip.

Alex reached the rear cabin and twisted off the canteen's top. The remainder of the water was warm, but he felt too guilty to pour it out. So he drank what was left in the canteen and filled it back with chilled water from the reservoir. From his front pocket, Alex pulled out the food pack that he'd saved from lunch. He opened the top and shook out a few peanuts into his hand. A good amount of salt fell out with the peanuts. He popped them in his mouth and ate them. Funny, peanuts weren't nuts at all. Peanuts were legumes and grew underground—not like true nuts. Nuts grow on trees and are contained in a hard shell.

Susan wasn't allergic to any other legume, or anything else, for that matter. Alex ate a few more nuts and drank from his canteen. It would have truly been a shame if Alex had been allergic to peanuts. Peanuts were about his favorite snack.

Alex brushed the salt from his hands and worked a piece of nut from between his teeth with is tongue. Then, he emptied the pack of nuts, and stuck the package in his shirt pocket.

*

The group of five had traveled just out of sight of the Warthog. Chief took the lead, and Ron brought up the rear. Ben had drifted away from Alex and Susan, and finally walked along side of Ron.

So far, Alex had only spotted a pterosaur resting in a tree. Now he wondered if the earlier group had frightened the wildlife away.

Susan basically acted like he wasn't there. Twenty years of marriage and right now he hardly even seemed to know who she was. It was a saddening thought. Two people that had once been so much in love they couldn't stand a minute apart, now couldn't stand a minute together. At least she wasn't making this trip worse by being mean to him. Of course, if she did have any interest in Chief, which Alex thought he gave more credence to than the reality of the situation, she wouldn't want to taint her image in front of him.

Susan came to a stop, raised her binoculars, and then headed toward a low-lying branch of a nearby tree.

She had obviously found something. Alex followed her and then looked and saw that Chief had come to a stop and was checking out the area. Ben was pointing up to a treetop, and Ron craned his head as if to see.

Susan snapped a couple of pictures of the tree trunk. She backed away when Alex arrived, and he saw what caught her eye. A tiny flower of some sort grew between the tree trunk and where the limb branched off. She stared at it like she was mesmerized by a precious jewel.

"It's beautiful," she said. "So tiny in a savage world of giants."

In that instant Susan transformed in Alex's eyes back to when they had first met—the carefree young woman who still believed in the magic of life—untainted by harsh cruelties of the world and the disappointments from the people who she loved. She was pretty back then, and she was almost that pretty now. Only the enchantment of youth was missing.

"Where did we go wrong, Susan?" Alex asked.

The serene expression disappeared from Susan's face as she narrowed her eyes toward him. "Really, you pick now to talk about something like this?"

"I just—"

"Spare me. This whole trip you haven't engaged me in two sentences of personal conversation—just like at home. We're out here to sightsee and get water. If you want to talk we can do that later on tonight. I'm around. I'm always around. You always find some excuse not to spend time with me."

The nostalgia of better times popped like a soap bubble. Would making the effort to save his marriage actually work? To do that, he'd have to break up with Natasha for good. He'd have to give up his passion for Cryptozoology—essentially killing the special things that gave him reasons to live now.

Alex nodded and saw that Chief was on the move again.

They had been gone nearly a half hour before Alex heard the mirth of the running creek. So far, if it hadn't been for pterosaurs nesting in trees, this excursion would have been a total bust for sightseeing. As it was, he was jaded to the winged reptiles by now.

Chief walked up to the side of the creek and scanned the area. He then removed his water backpack to begin filling it.

"Susan, stay with me a minute," Alex said, and grabbed Susan's hand.

She looked at him, her brow furrowing.

Alex waited for Ron and Ben to pass and reach the creek's bank, which was about ten yards away, before he continued to speak. "I just want to say this. I really did love you—back in the beginning. I still held on to that love as I pursued my passion for Cryptozoology, and you did everything you could to kill my dreams. I want you to know that I harbor the same type of love now as I did then. I want to be happy, and I want you to be happy. I am going to do what it takes to make sure we both find that happiness in life." Alex wrapped his arms around Susan and gave her a big hug. He looked over and saw the other three filling their water backpacks.

Ben looked back and gave him a sly smile and a nod.

Alex gave Susan a long kiss and released his embrace.

"Alex . . . I wasn't expecting that," she said, a little out of breath. Her mouth hung slightly open, and then her lips formed a shy smile.

Alex winked and removed his canteen from his belt, opened the top, and drank. He handed Susan the canteen.

She brushed the hair away from the side of her face and took a swallow. Her nose scrunched in obvious disgust. "This tastes salty."

Alex shrugged his shoulders and took the canteen.

"Come on. I need to fill my backpack." Alex turned and took a few steps before he heard Susan gag, but didn't stop.

Then he heard a loud gasp as she struggled to breathe. The raspy sound was loud enough for Chief and the others by the creek to look his way.

Alex turned in time to see his wife's mouth contorted in a silent scream as she fell to the ground, her body flailing.

"Susan!" Alex hollered. He let the backpack drop from his shoulders and rushed to her side. "Susan! Susan! Help!"

Chief was the first to arrive and slid down beside her. "What is it? What's happening?"

"I don't know! She can't breathe! She's having a seizure!" Alex said in a panic.

Susan frothed at the mouth, and her lips were swollen. Her face began to lose color and then it bloomed soft lavender.

Chief immediately started CPR, having no luck forcing a breath into her lungs.

"Her Epi-Pen! It's in the front cabin!" Alex stood as if to retrieve it.

"Stay here! I'll get it!" Ben shouted as he turned and ran for the Warthog.

"Oh, my God, Susan!" Alex hyperventilated.

Ron laid his hand on Alex's should. "Chief's got her. It's going to be okay. It's going to be okay."

Chief frantically did everything he could to save Susan from dying. The end came quickly. Her body stopped shaking as if she was being electrocuted and the power had been suddenly shut off.

The field medic continued CPR far longer than Alex thought necessary. In the frenzy, he heard some of Susan's ribs crack during chest compressions.

Exhausted, Chief fell on his back and struggled to fill his lungs with air.

Alex leaned over Susan, pressing his cheek to hers, and cried uncontrollably.

"I'm sorry. I'm so sorry," Ron said in a whisper, patting the grieving man on the back.

*

"Natasha, what happened to your arm?" Matt said, pointing to her left forearm.

She raised her arm and peered down. "Yeah, I scraped it on a tree on the trip this morning. I had forgotten about it. It's okay."

"Yeah, but we shouldn't take any chances," Matt said, and then headed into the front cabin. "Who knows what kind of bacteria we're dealing with out here," he spoke loud enough for her to hear.

"You're right," Natasha said.

Matt stepped out of the front cabin, carrying an alcohol wipe and an adhesive bandage. He ripped the antiseptic open using his teeth to hold the package in place and pulled out the wipe. "This might sting a bit."

"I'm a big girl. It'll be okay," Natasha said.

"Yeah, too bad I don't have a sucker to give you afterward." Matt gently wiped the wound.

Logan walked in under the canopy. He stopped and bit his lower lip. "What's going on?"

"The great huntress has an *owie*," Matt said.

"Is it bad?" Logan asked.

"It's just a scratch. Nothing to worry about," Natasha said.

"You wouldn't be saying that if you had broken a nail," Logan said.

Natasha giggled. "You're right about that."

Right after Matt applied the bandage, his satellite phone rang. "What the . . . ?"

Natasha and Logan turned wary gazes his way. Matt unclipped the phone from his belt, and answered, "Hello."

"There's . . . there's been an accident . . ."

Matt knew by the sound of the voice that it was Chief. And from the tone, he knew something bad had happened.

"Okay, how bad is it?" Matt asked.

His words squeezed expressions of alarm on his two friends' faces.

"The Professor's wife . . . Susan. She had some kind of episode . . . reaction. I don't know. She couldn't breathe . . . I couldn't save her."

"Oh, God . . . no." Matt lowered his gaze. Susan, dead. *Poor Alex, he must be going through hell.*

"What happened?" Natasha asked through trembling lips.

"Ben's heading back to get an Epi-Pen. Tell him it's too late. Everyone just stay there. We'll bring her in. Tell the others. I called you because you need to be there for Alex. He's pretty shook up."

"I understand," Matt said. The phone call ended. He lowered the phone by his side. "Susan had an attack——"

"She was attacked!" Natasha cried out.

Matt raised his hand. "No, she wasn't attacked. She had some type of *attack*—reaction . . . she stopped breathing and . . ." Matt choked up on his last word. Tears welled in his eyes, and doing his best to utter the words, he said, "She didn't make it."

"Son-of-a-bitch," Logan whispered.

"Oh no, that's terrible . . . Poor Alex," Natasha said, and brought her hands over her mouth.

"Hey! Hey!" Ben called, his voice faint in the distance.

"Ben's coming for the Epi-Pen . . . He doesn't know," Matt said. He turned and exited the doorway leading out the canopied area. Logan and Natasha followed.

Meat was on watch and had his rifle at the ready. He turned as Matt approached, and said, "Something's up."

"Yeah. There's been a death. Susan," Matt said.

Meat shook his head.

"She wasn't killed. She had some kind of reaction and couldn't breathe," Matt said.

Ben sprang into view from behind a tree, and in his haste, forgot to watch his footing. A root caught his ankle, and he hit the ground hard.

By this time Caveman had joined with rifle in hand. "What's after him?"

"Logan, you and Natasha stay here. Tell him. I'll see about Ben," Matt said, and trotted off to his fallen friend, who struggled to stand.

"Hold on, Ben," Matt said.

"Get the Epi-Pen! Susan's having an attack!" Ben cried through struggling breaths.

Matt ran up to Ben and held on to his elbow, as the young man tried to stand on wobbly legs. "Ben. Calm down. It's . . . it's too late."

"Wha—How do you know?" Ben asked, and shook his head.

"Chief called . . . said he couldn't save her," Matt said.

"No. Oh, no. Jesus Christ on a stick . . ." Ben dropped his gaze to the ground.

"You okay?" Meat had arrived.

"I think so—SHIT!" Ben had tried unsuccessfully to put his weight on his foot.

"Come on, let's get you back to camp," Matt said.

"But what about Susan?" Ben asked.

"They're bringing her back. They'll be here shortly. We need to be ready for Alex," Matt said. He and Meat placed an arm under Ben's shoulders and helped him back to camp.

*

It wasn't long before Chief came into view from the forest.

Alex followed close behind, carrying Susan in his arms. Her arms hung down—dead weight, and her head was back and mouth opened. Vacant eyes stared at the vapor canopy above. It was as gruesome a sight as it was sad.

The receiving crew waited near the Warthog. Matt stood apart from the group in front, with Natasha and Logan just behind him to either side.

All life had drained from Alex's face. He looked like a zombie functioning on pure instinct. His face was dirty—smeared from tears—and had some mucous looking substance on his chin and shirt.

Matt didn't know what to say. What could you say that just wouldn't sound so simple? *I'm sorry for you loss. I know how you must feel. She's in a better place.* It all sounded like pandering bullshit to express the sorrow he had for his friend. He turned his head to the side, and said to Logan, "Go get something to lay Susan's body on—and something to cover it with too."

Chief walked past Matt, only turning his gaze up at him for a brief moment before heading to the Warthog. The man truly looked upset. Chief had said, 'I couldn't save her,' in the earlier conversation. There was the possibility the field medic blamed himself.

Alex approached, his head hanging low.

"Oh, Alex. I'm so sorry. This, uh . . . this is horrible," Matt said, stiffing his jaw so it wouldn't quiver. He didn't want to cry. He wanted to stay strong for Alex's sake.

Alex grimaced, his eyes squeezed tightly, and his mouth widened as his teeth clenched together—holding back tears.

"Alex. Let me take Susan," Matt said, and waited for Alex to comply.

"I'll take her." Ron had been standing behind Alex and came around in front. He gently took the dead woman from the Professor's arms, not waiting for permission.

Matt walked up to Alex and hugged him.

Tear's broke and Alex cried. When he recovered a bit, he said, "I couldn't do anything to save her. I should have brought her medicine with us. I should have——"

"You can't blame yourself over this," Matt said. "It had been over an hour since Susan ate. There was no reason to think she'd need her medicine. She must have reacted to some mold or fungus here. There was no way you could have known. She didn't consider it either."

"Yes, but had I brought the antihistamines she'd be alive right now."

"You don't know that, Alex. Look, you can't blame yourself. You didn't do anything wrong. Let's get you cleaned up a bit. Get some water and get into the cool of the front cabin. We can talk some more later."

Alex shook his head, and the two walked toward the rear cabin.

Natasha waited with her arms folded across her chest.

"Go and get Alex a clean shirt," he told her.

She nodded and sped off.

When they made it to the rear cabin, Matt wet a rag by the water valve, and handed it to Alex.

The professor removed his hat and wiped his face. "Thanks. That does feel better."

Natasha arrived with a fresh shirt. "Here, put this on."

Alex unbuttoned his shirt, and Matt took the old one from him.

"Thanks for getting my shirt, Natasha," Alex said, and wiped the back of his neck with the rag before putting on the shirt.

"Here, come with me." She took two bottles of water from the cooler, grabbed Alex by the hand, and whisked him away.

Matt was momentarily stunned by Natasha's abrupt maneuver. Alex needed a friend right now to give him strength. Not a shoulder to cry on and wallow in sorrow. He watched the two depart hand in hand, and a strange feeling crept over him—the same feeling he had when Alex helped teach Natasha how to shoot. Something looked out of place, but he couldn't put his finger on it.

Matt still had Alex's shirt in his hand. He grabbed it at the collar and began to fold it when something *crinkled* in the front pocket.

Matt poked his fingers in the pocket and removed a generic looking food packet. It was clearly marked: Peanuts.

CHAPTER 15

"Roll Tide!" Don said with gusto after he had sipped from the bottle of Scotch whiskey.

The Mule had been traveling for more than six hours. Coop's ass started to miss the more comfortable seats in the Warthog. At least the ATTC was roomy enough to stand and walk around. One thing for sure, just as soon as they returned to the United States, he was going to see the doctor and do something about those hemorrhoids. For now, Advil and a frequent application of Preparation H would have to suffice.

"You want some?" Don sat in the front passenger seat and had asked Coop, the driver.

"Yes, I *want* some. But *no*, I'm going to wait until we set up camp for the night. I can't take any chances out here with so much riding on the line."

"Hey, it's thirsty back here," Suge said. He and Bats had drawn the short straw for the rear seats.

Don took a furtive hit from the bottle before passing it back.

They had made good time once they left the Warthog. The Forest thinned out a few miles from departure. The area opened into an Africa-like plain. Scrubby grass and sparsely growing trees allowed the Mule to travel at top speed.

It had been a few hours since they had seen life of any kind, though the GPS map showed that was about to quickly change. In less than an hour they'd reach the bend in Lear's river that neared their destination. He'd wished his crew would have held out from hitting the bottle until after they passed the potential threat. But even Coop was subject to peer pressure, and his crew ragged him enough for him to give in. He'd be sure to put a stop to it before things got out of hand.

Coop's satellite phone, clipped in his belt, buzzed. He looked at the time on the dash and cast a wary glace at Don. "We check back in another half hour. Something's up if they couldn't wait."

He retrieved his phone, and answered, "Coop here. What's up?"

"Got some bad news." It was Chief's voice.

"Hold on. I'm putting you on speaker," Coop said, and pushed the phone's screen. "Go ahead."

"Susan Klasse had some kind of allergic reaction. Her throat closed up—couldn't breathe. We couldn't save her," Chief said.

"Damn." Coop pounded the steering wheel with his fist and slowed the Mule to a stop. "Was it something she ate? Hell, she brought her own food. I didn't expect this to happen."

"Happened more than an hour after she ate—don't think it was food related. It must have been something airborne. Bacteria, yeasts, who knows? Doesn't matter. Dead is dead."

"Dead is dead," Bats said matter-of-factly.

"You're right. Dead is dead." Coop huffed out a breath of bad air. "How's the professor dealing with it?"

"He's upset, of course. Mostly in shock. I gave him a couple of painkillers to help him deal with it. But you know how all this works. It's going to take time for him to go through all the phases of loss," Chief said.

Yes, Coop knew all too well the winding road of grief. "How's he acting? Is he ready to throw in the towel and leave? Give his wife a *proper* burial and all that bullshit?"

"No, he hasn't said anything like that," Chief said.

"Chief, you know we're not going back until our mission is complete."

"Yes, I know that."

"I need you to convince the professor that the best thing we can do under the circumstances is to bury his wife here. We have no way to preserve her body and bring it back two weeks from now. Can you do that?" Coop asked.

"I can try my best. If he won't listen, I won't give him any other choice. He may not like it, but he will have to accept it," Chief said.

"Take pictures of the body. There'll be legal issues to deal with once we get back to the States. Get witness statements right now on video," Coop said.

"I was there, and I took pictures right after it happened. I'll get the statements."

"Good. Have John and Meat on their best behavior—maybe have them keep a little distance from the professor until after the burial. We don't want to upset Alex for no reason. Have some type of service and make sure you bury that body as deep as you can. Wrap a tarp around it—throw some latrine chemicals on it—we don't want to attract any carrion eaters. Just don't let Alex see you do anything disrespectful to the body. He might lose it."

"Roger that, Coop. Everything good on your end?" Chief asked.

"Smooth sailing so far. We should be more than halfway there by nightfall. Call you back in a couple," Coop said.

"Roger, out."

Coop terminated the call and placed his phone back on his belt. "Well, isn't that a lovely pile of horseshit."

"You mean dinosaur-shit, don't you?" Bats said, sounding more drunk than what Coop reasoned.

He turned his head toward the backseat and saw that the Scotch bottle was half empty. "Give me that."

Bats surrendered the bottle.

Coop wiped the top with his hand and took a mouthful. Not the most dignified way in the world to enjoy such a fine bottle of spirits, but none of that mattered right now. He handed Don the bottle. "Put the top back on. We'll have it later."

"Sure thing," Don said.

The Mule's tracks began moving and soon reached full speed.

"She wasn't a bad looking woman. A little older than me. I've had worse," Bats said.

"Yeah, but she always had that sour look on her face. Something was stuck up her ass," Coop said.

"Except when Chief was around," Suge said, and followed with a chuckle.

"The woman's dead. Show her some respect," Don said, his bottom lip pushed his mouth into a frown.

"Maybe Don was a little sweet on her, too, and we didn't realize it," Bats said, and reached over and stuck his finger in Don's left ear.

Don flinched and slapped Bats' hand. "Come on, guys. This ain't some raghead that died for not being an American. This is a woman we're talking about. I ain't never had a wife, and I just think it's turrible she died."

"We didn't think you needed a wife because you had Ron," Bats said, and laughed.

Don slowly turned around, and with half closed eyes, peered at Bats. "Boy, you keep that up, and I'm going to whip that ass. And when we get back to the Warthog, Ron's gonna kick that ass even worse."

"Okay, don't make me stop this car and make you two sit in time out. Sheesh. I thought you guys could hold your booze better than that," Coop said.

"Booze is just a poor substitute for what ails me. I need to kill something," Bats said.

"You may just get your chance real soon," Coop said. He had the roof mounted .50 caliber's camera zoomed in to the southwest. "The GPS shows an oxbow lake less than a mile from here. You can see trees growing by it on the screen."

Bats and Suge leaned their heads in between Coop's and Don's for a clearer view.

"There's bound to be something there. Hopefully not any big nasties. We can't avoid the area. The terrain slightly to the east has a big drop off. The Mule's fast enough to outrun anything we might have a problem killing," Coop said.

"Look, there's a herd of something in front of the trees. They're brown and green. That's those Triceratopses like we saw before," Suge said.

"Yeah. They probably won't bother us as long as we don't fuck with them. I'm going to slow down a bit in case they get spooked. I'd hate to be going sixty miles an hour and them to get scared and run in front of us," Coop said.

"You think we should fire a few rounds from the fifty?" Don asked.

"No, let's see how they react. I need as much information as I can get about the indigenous life for my report."

The Mule slowed and approached within 50 yards of the Triceratops herd. This bunch was of the same species as the ones they viewed on the drone's video. Even from this distance, Coop noticed how massive they were compared to humans. Alex had told him prehistoric Triceratops stood at twice the height of a man and were nearly ten men standing side by side with arms out in length. The professor also wondered if the Triceratops, and other dinosaurs in Patagonia for that matter, might be smaller in size because of the lower oxygen percentage in today's atmosphere. The oxygen rich atmosphere in prehistoric times allowed dragonflies to grow just short of two feet in length. Right now, Coop didn't believe lower oxygen levels mattered. These dinosaurs were fucking huge.

"Pull on over," Bats said.

"What for?" Coop asked.

"Aw, come on. Pull on over so we can get a better look," Bats said.

"Yeah," Suge added.

"All right. Let's bug out at the first sign of trouble, though." Coop slowed the Mule to a stop and set the brake.

The two doors to either side of the Mule opened, and the four men made their exit.

Coop slowed his pace so he could stealthily scratch his ass—the sensitive nether region crying for a fresh application of Preparation H.

Don had his field glasses out and scanned the area. Suge had grabbed two rifles from the back and handed one to Bats, who used the rifle's scope to spy on the Triceratopses.

"Damn. Look at those things. They even make a buffalo look small. You ever seen a buffalo?" Bats said.

Suge stepped beside him and raised his rifle. "Can't say that I have." He took a long look through the scope and lowered the gun.

"Uh oh. Looks like one of them bull's spotted us," Don said.

Coop walked up next to Don and looked through his field glasses. "Yep, and it's either mad, curious, or both."

"I've heard buffalos are blind. These things certainly aren't blind if they can see us at this distance," Bats said.

The animal lumbered in their direction. It didn't approach with caution, and it wasn't in a raging charge either. Perhaps it was just curious. Better to not stick around and find out.

"Okay guys, lets head out," Coop said.

"What for? There's only one," Bats said.

"So, we need to leave."

"But I thought you needed information for your research?" Bats said.

"I do, so—"

"So we need to know what it takes to kill one of these things," Bats said.

"Are you nuts?"

"Maybe, but if you find a shit-load of diamonds and a larger expedition wants to come back, you better have some hard data to prove what it takes to protect them," Bats said.

As crazy as the man might have been, he certainly had a point. Coop thought a bit, and since it was only one bull, it was worth the risk to see how a Seven rifle would fare against a Triceratops. If not, they still had the .50 caliber on the roof. It was powerful enough to take down a herd of elephants. Coop believed it could handle one Triceratops.

"Don, go in the Mule, and zero in the fifty cal. Wait for my orders before firing," Coop said.

Don did as ordered, and Coop stood alongside of Bats. "Okay, let's see what we can do."

"You're on," Bats said. A rare smile curled on his lips. He raised his rifle. "That's a big bastard." The rifle fired, the blast suppressed by the Seven's custom barrel. A .308 caliber bullet found its target on its chest just under the beast's head. The special tip exploded on impact.

Coop saw the flash of the explosion and a fist sized crater on the Triceratops' chest.

The mighty creature cried in pain or surprise. The cry sounded like the baritone of a metallic horn. The others in the herd took quick notice, freezing in position, and raising heads cautiously in the air.

"Guys, if the herd comes to the rescue get ready to run," Coop said.

Bats fired again, knocking another chunk of meat out next to the first. "I don't think I'm getting much penetration."

"It's not slowing him down either," Suge said.

"Going with the rocket," Bats said. The side rocket launched and struck its target, knocking the beast to the ground. The rocket's blast on impact sent the Triceratops herd scurrying in the other direction.

"Survival of the fittest or the smartest," Coop said.

The downed Triceratops brayed like an injured cow. The animal still lived and was suffering.

"Shit," Coop said.

"You want me to try the grenades? See what kind of damage they'll do?" Bats asked.

"No. I think they have tiny brains, and with all that armor on its head, you might have to blow it clean off to kill it. We need to stop the heart." Coop turned to Don. "The animal's on its side, you got the shot?"

"Yeah. No problem," Don said.

"Do it."

The machine gun rattled several armor piercing rounds into the Triceratops' chest. Its left leg raised and shook, and then the animal became deathly still. From all indications it was dead.

"Good shooting," Coop said, and then scanned the area to see if the gunfire had attracted any other dinosaurs ready to defend its territory. The Triceratops herd had disappeared into the forest.

Bats walked at a quick pace to check out the prize.

Suge turned to Coop, who nodded. The two men followed, with Don close on their heels.

The dinosaur looked as big as a short school bus. Surprisingly, its skin looked like a hybrid of reptile and mammal skin. Sort of like a cross between elephant and iguana. It had its own distinct musk, but wasn't much different from what you would smell at a stockyard. It was at this point Coop surmised that some of the large clumps on the ground were dinosaur droppings.

"It's got red blood . . . and look at the meat," Bats said, poking the chest wound with his survival knife. "It's red meat."

"Yeah. Alex told me new theories supported that dinosaurs were warm blooded, red meat animals. In fact, I didn't realize this, but mammals evolved from reptiles," Coop said.

"Wow. I didn't know that either," Suge said. "Makes you think."

"Yeah, think what?" Coop asked.

"You know. Man's a mammal. We went from monkeys to apes to human somehow. Well, some dinosaurs already walked on two legs. That was millions of years ago. Why didn't they evolve into something like man?"

"You mean like lizard people that fly UFOs?" Don asked.

"I know what you getting at, Don. So, yeah. Something like that," Suge said.

"Interesting question. Don't know. Who knows what turns the wheels of evolution? There's a theory that an asteroid struck the Earth millions of years ago and killed off the dinosaurs. Maybe they would have become man-like had that not happened."

"Coop. Take my picture," Bats said. He stood next to the Triceratops' head and posed like a big game hunter.

"Wait, I want in," Don said.

"Me too," Suge said.

The three men moved in position while Alex unclipped his phone and brought it before him to frame the photo. "Okay, wait . . . let me zoom in . . . Suge, move a little closer to Bats. That's it. Hold still, and I'll take a few." Coop clicked off five shots. "There. Got it."

"Boy, those animal rights nut-jobs are going to be some upset when they see a picture of this," Suge said.

"Yeah, and that's why our job is for them *never* to see it. Remember, we're all under contract," Coop said.

"What're we gonna do now? That head mounted on the wall would make me the most popular man in Alabama, but it's too big to bring back with us," Don said.

"That would make one hell of a trophy." Coop laughed. "Say, you got me thinking. People pay big money to hunt, right?"

"Yep," Don said.

"So, what would someone pay to kill a dinosaur? I mean, not here, of course. But if we can put these things on a ranch somewhere—breed them. Make it all on the up and up. I bet some people would pay a million dollars to kill one of these and have the head for a trophy."

"Hell, maybe more. You get one of those rich pro athletes to kill one and all his other buddies are going to have to kill one too. Dinosaur trophies will become the new bling," Suge said.

"And Ace Corp will take all their money. I'm definitely putting this in my report," Coop said.

"All I know is that I ain't had a good steak in a while. I'm going to carve off some back-strap, and find the tenderloin and cut it out. We're going to eat like kings tonight," Don said.

"I'll drink to that. Beats the hell out of a MRE," Coop said. His imagination drifted to a remote area in Montana, with rolling green hills, and snowcapped mountains on the horizon. He's the proprietor of the lodge, entertaining the world's elite after a successful dinosaur hunt. Smoking cigars by the roaring fireplace while telling soldier of fortune stories and being one of the first to discover prehistoric creatures still roamed the Earth. His mouth widened into a smile so large he thought his lips were going to split.

CHAPTER 16

Chief terminated the call to Coop, picked up his cap, and rubbed the hand still holding the phone across his brow. It's not like he hadn't anticipated some sort of accident on this trip. He even considered death a probable possibility. But he thought that more so of Coop and the three others who headed off on their own, away from the protection of the Warthog.

His main job was to keep the college crew safe from harm. And even if that meant they had to spend the entire trip holed up inside the Warthog, so be it. Of course, Chief didn't wish for such a scenario. Part of him was as excited as they were to witness the precious gift time had saved for them.

So far, the dangers had been few, and he was ready to explore farther into the forest. A waterfall was less than two miles away, and for tomorrow he had planned a northeasterly trip to put them near it. If all went well, the following day he'd lead them to the waterfall.

Now all those plans had to be scratched. At least, he'd put things on hold for one day. Chief figured they'd bury Susan this afternoon, take tomorrow off as a day of mourning, and test the spirit of the crew the day after. If Alex didn't want to come, that was fine. The college kids were manageable. They had proven to be a lot more useful than what he had originally imagined.

Chief had grown rather fond of Ben. More from a distance than any direct contact. Now that the young man was injured, his left ankle sprained so badly Chief was surprised he could even walk, he'd be in charge of base camp if and when another expedition went out.

Chief planned on teaching Ben how to use the big gun on the Warthog's roof later today. The young man already knew how to drive the ATTC. He should be more than capable to handle the modified .50 caliber machine gun.

Ron, Meat, and Caveman waited for him in front of the Warthog.

Chief had walked the short distance from where he made the phone call, and said, "We've got our orders. I've already taken pictures of the deceased. Ron, I'll be taking a video statement of the account later on."

"Roll Tide," Ron said.

"We're going to bury the body—as soon as we can. I'm going to break the news to the professor as soon as I leave. That means we need a hole dug as deep as practical. Just south of the rear cabin, there's a rocky area. See if you can find some soft ground near it. Dig the hole there, because we'll cover the grave with rocks to keep scavengers away," Chief said.

"What about the rest of the mission? Is Coop going to allow us to go out, or are we confined in house until his team gets back?" Meat asked.

"I have no plans to change the agenda because a woman died from a nut allergy. I'm not sure how the professor will spend his time, and I really don't care how he does. The thought of staying cooped up around here with my finger up my ass is enough to make me want to cut my wrist. For once, I feel like I'm on an adventure, not just doing a job. That may sound unprofessional, selfish, juvenile—I don't give a fuck. I have a feeling this trip is going to change my life forever. I think it will change *all* our lives."

"Yeah, I think you're right," Meat said. "In a few years, when our contract ends and we can talk about the trip, we'll be as big as rock stars."

"You know what? I'm the first human being ever to eat a dinosaur egg! That ranks right up there with the first man that walked on the moon. They's gonna put me in the *Guinness Book of World Records*," Caveman said.

"Or in jail," Meat said.

"Okay, guys. Let's get moving. Coop said we should wrap the body in a tarp and use latrine chemicals to help mask the odor. We won't do that to the body until we get the professor out of the way. We'll have a short memorial and move on. We'll lay low tomorrow, but come the next day, it's business as usual," Chief said, and headed for the front cabin.

The other three turned to start their assignment.

*

Chief entered the front cabin and saw Ben sitting, his left leg propped across the bench, and his crutches within reach. Chief was glad someone had the wherewithal to pack a set of crutches for this trip.

Logan and Matt sat on the same bench as Ben. Logan looked as antsy as an expectant father, but Matt had his arms crossed over his chest and cast a wary gaze with his head cocked to one side.

Alex lied on his sleeping bag, awake, but despondent.

Natasha sat on the floor by Alex's side. She gently held a damp rag on his forehead.

Chief paused a moment and ran his fingers over his mouth and down his chin. He spoke calmly, "Alex. Are you good to talk?"

The professor slowly turned his gaze toward Chief. "Yeah. I'm good."

"I know this is a tough time, but there are some important matters we have to take care of," Chief said.

"Okay."

"Alex, we aren't going to be able to bring Susan's body back with us," Chief said.

"But we have an ice machine in the rear cabin. Can't we keep her iced down until we get back?" Ben asked.

"That won't work, Ben. The ice we make is in small cubes. You know how quickly it melts. You'd need block commercial ice to preserve a body," Chief said, slightly pissed from the distraction. "Alex, we need to bury Susan. And we need to do it this afternoon."

"This afternoon?" Alex said.

"Yes. I'm sure you're aware how fast a body decomposes. Uh, you know how a body misshapes—giving off gasses as cells die. I . . . I just think it would be better for you if your last memory of seeing Susan is one where she would look as lovely as you remember her," Chief said, hoping his bedside demeanor didn't sound too contrived.

Alex turned his gaze to the ceiling but didn't say a word.

"It's hot outside, and the heat only makes things worse. My men are preparing the gravesite now. We can have a memorial—

say a few words in her honor." Chief had made the pitch. He hoped things didn't have to get ugly.

"Alex, it's what's best for you," Natasha said.

"It is . . . it is," Alex said, then turned his head toward Chief, and gave a slight nod.

"It's going to be okay, Alex. We'll all help you through this," Chief said, and then stepped out the front cabin.

*

Matt sat under the shade of a tall tree while he watched Caveman feed a Compsognathus some type of meat from one of Susan's MREs. Feeding a dinosaur food bombarded with preservatives and chemicals was wrong on so many levels. Right now, he didn't give a fuck.

About this time the day before, Susan Klasse had been laid to rest. For some reason he had expected the event to carry a greater sadness. Maybe it would have if more people had become emotional. Susan had died without warning, and before rigor mortis had fully set in, she was in the ground and covered. Even when Alex said a few departing words her death seemed surreal— almost as if they were all in a play and had to finish their part so they could move on. But no one got emotional. No one shed one single tear, not even Alex, and Matt knew why.

"Hey, buddy. What are you doing out here by your lonesome?" Logan said, arriving to his side.

"Oh, hey. I didn't see you coming. I'm . . . I'm just out here . . . thinking. You know."

"Yeah, I know," Logan said, and then sat next to Matt. He crossed his legs and patted a hand gently on his knee. "I can't believe Susan's gone."

"It's weird. We saw her less than an hour before she died—she sat right across from me. Then, we find out she's dead." Those thoughts were true, and he was willing to share them with Logan. Telling his friend that he'd found the empty peanut pack was another story. On one hand he wanted to, but once that cat got out of the bag, it could never go back in again. Right now wasn't the proper time to create such a shit-storm. Alex was his friend. Was his *friend* a murderer? All evidence seemed to point that way. But why? Especially, why here, and why now? Maybe the answer had been in front of him the whole time, and he was too stupid to see.

"And now, it's like Susan never even existed," Logan said. "The headstone Ron made with the laser was pretty cool."

"It was," Matt said. He picked up a leaf off the ground and pretended to examine it. "Alex seems to be taking the death in stride. I . . . Natasha's been with him in the front cabin all day. I've gone in and checked on him a few times. Each time I go in, the room seems to ice up. I feel out of place—like I'm in the way."

Logan cleared his throat and looked off into the distance.

"I'm picking up some strange vibes. Natasha's acting *really* familiar around Alex. She slept by his side last night, you know."

Logan kept his gaze away from Matt. "Yeah, I know."

Matt watched Logan squirm a bit and felt there was something his friend knew that he didn't. "Logan."

"What?" He looked down to the ground.

"Is something going on between Natasha and Alex?"

Logan blew some air from between his lips. He turned his head up, and said, "Yeah . . . Yeah there is."

"You . . . knew?"

"Yeah, well . . . didn't know for sure for a while. But I know now they've been seeing each other for a good amount of time," Logan said.

He had not known Logan to be anything but truthful to him, or anyone else, for that matter. Logan spoke as if he were a bit unsure of himself.

"Look, I knew you had feelings for her. In fact, you two seemed to be getting closer. I was thinking Natasha might just end it with Alex and the whole thing would take care of itself. I didn't want your feelings to get hurt. We're friends. You know I care about you."

That was true, for sure. Logan had proven time and time again to be his most reliable friend. In fact, Matt's busy life had pushed many of his old friends out of the picture. Next to Alex, he was closer to Logan than anyone else.

"Yeah, man. I understand, and I'm thankful to have a friend like you." Matt reached over and patted Logan's thigh a couple of times.

A boyish grin was Logan's only reply.

"We're going out again tomorrow. Chief says we'll be checking the area near the waterfall," Matt said.

"Yeah. I'm hoping everything goes okay. I so want to see the waterfall," Logan said. "You, uh, you think Alex is going to come with us?"

"Yes, oh yes," Matt said and slowly nodded. "He'll be right there next to Natasha. I just hope he doesn't have his nose so far up her ass that he'll miss seeing anything."

CHAPTER 17

They next day after breakfast, everyone but Ben headed out to explore the adjoining area. Matt saw the disappointment on Ben's face before they left, but the young athlete did his best to hide his feelings with his encouraging words. Logan even offered to stay behind with him, but Ben would have none of that. He just forced a smile and ensured everyone that he was good.

Chief had taught him how to use the remote to fire the Warthog's machine gun. The gun could be operated from on top or remotely. The deadly weapon had been loaded with armor piercing ammo.

The journey had the expedition following the creek and heading north from where Susan died. So far, about the only wildlife they'd seen were the small to medium sized pterosaurs, residing in the upper regions of the trees. Matt remembered Alex saying they hadn't seen near the variety of wildlife when they made their trip to get water the day before yesterday. Humans invading the area may have scared the indigenous life away. Imagine that. Prehistoric animals had enough instinct to realize the deadly threat man presented.

Trees randomly grew near the bank. The breeze rustled leaves and the water babbled trickling over rocks in the creek. There was enough brush for wildlife to hide, and Matt stayed on the constant lookout for it.

He remembered a time, back in his college days, he and a group of friends had hiked through the everglades. Matt rounded a tree and surprised an armadillo. The armored mammal screeched and flew into the air what seemed like three feet, as if propelled by a spring. Matt had screamed too, just as startled. Unfortunately, one of his buddies was close enough to witness his freak out. And, of course, his friends harassed him over it the rest of the trip and a long time afterward.

The group had come to a halt while Chief looked at data on his satellite phone. During the whole trip, everyone had stayed not much more than an arm's length apart. Except for, as he had predicted, Natasha and Alex. The overt public displays of affection between them had rage boiling inside. Did Natasha know Alex killed Susan? Was she in on it too? An even worse thought, was it Natasha's idea?

A pterosaur in a nearby tree flapped its wing, grunted a *caw* of sorts, and flew away. Watching a winged lizard take flight was marvelous to witness. Matt brought his video camera up and filmed what he could before the creature became lost in the treetops.

The satellite phone on Matt's belt buzzed. He retrieved it, and answered, "Hey."

"Hey," Ben said. "Any action out there?"

"Not so far—except for the creek. There're crocs in the water, so we have to keep a little bit of a distance. The one I saw must have been over thirty feet long."

"That's a lot of boots," Ben said, and chuckled. "So, what are y'all going to do now?"

"I don't know. Maybe we'll take another path back to the Warthog and hopefully see something else. Chief's playing with his phone. Maybe he's plotting a course."

"Okay, I'll let you go. I call back in an hour if I don't hear from you. Bye," Ben said.

"See you." Matt ended the call.

"Alex, can you step over here? You can see the screen better in the shade," Chief said, his gaze turned toward his phone.

The professor complied with Natasha glued to his hip.

Before the couple reached Chief, Meat called out, "Natasha, come see."

Matt looked over and saw Meat, Ron, Caveman, and Logan about twenty feet away. They had found something, but why Meat had only called Natasha over was a bit of a mystery.

"I want to go over our next plan of action," Chief said as Alex reached his side. "Matt, you want to come over?"

"Sure," Matt said, feeling a bit honored that Chief included him in the hierarchy of decision-making.

"Look at the size of that flower!" Natasha said.

Matt and the two men beside him turned gazes toward Meat and Caveman, who had pulled some foliage aside, exposing a huge red and pink flower. The bloom looked as big as Natasha's head.

"Come stand next to it. I want to take your picture," Meat said to Natasha.

"Okay," Chief continued. "We can—"

Another pterosaur flapped its wings in a nearby tree and flew off uttering an ear-piercing shriek.

"Damn, that was loud," Matt said, and cast his gaze around. Something about the situation didn't feel right.

Chief looked up from his phone, narrowing his eyes has he looked curiously about. A few moments passed, and he continued, "So, the waterfall is about a half mile north. I had originally planned to move the Warthog closer before venturing that far away. But since things are pretty dead around here, I don't have any problem with going the distance today. Thoughts?"

Before he or Alex had a chance to answer, the air filled with cries of various species of pterosaurs. Similar to a flock of birds fleeing in mass exodus, the winged lizards took flight.

Everyone in the group had frozen in position, only their heads turning to watch the startled reptiles.

Chief put his phone away and slowly removed his rifle off his shoulder. "I don't like this," he said loud enough for everyone to hear.

Matt didn't like it, either. All of a sudden it was as though the breeze had stopped and the air had become more humid. It was probably all in his imagination, but something inside, maybe something primordial, raised the hair on the back of his neck.

There was some rustling on the ground coming from the east.

Chief raised his left hand and pointed. The other Redwater members moved their rifles to the ready.

Then Matt heard something. It almost sounded like a mixture of a growl and a purr.

Two theropods, both slightly larger than men, sprang from around brush, and dashed straight for the middle of the group.

These creatures had hunger in their eyes and sharp talons on the end of their claws. They were greenish yellow in color, with the bellies several shades lighter than the rest. The head reminded

Matt of a cross between an ostrich and a lizard. They had rows of pointed teeth and jaws that looked like they could bend steel.

"Take 'em down!" Chief ordered.

The JNY-7s rattled out ordnance, striking the attacking creatures, and blowing chunks of flesh into the air on impact.

"Troodons!" Alex yelled. "Look, there's more!"

Several others sprang out and headed straight for them. The rifles had slowed both of the original attackers which fought to keep moving forward in the barrage of bullets. They were probably dead but didn't know it. Getting a headshot to immediately drop them seemed almost impossible.

By this time Matt and Alex had their .45s out and had squeezed off a few rounds of their own. There was no way to know if either had found the target.

The lead Troodons hit the ground not ten feet from Matt. Some of the others had slowed their advance a bit, while a contingency of six continued the Blitzkrieg.

"They're trying to split the group!" Chief called.

Matt realized Chief was right. The Troodons were attempting to wedge between him, Alex, and Chief—cutting the three of them off from the group. They were being hunted just like the Velociraptors hunted the Triceratops—trimming a few from the herd.

"I'm out of bullets!" Alex cried.

Matt's slide racked back and remained open. He was out of ammo too. They both had spare magazines on their belts, but Matt didn't see the use in reloading, and Alex must have forgotten in the panic.

The rifles brought down more of the Troodons, but those in waiting weren't scared off and continued to advance.

By this time one or more of the Redwater crew had launched a few grenades, blasting Troodons parts about the area. How many were in this herd? Matt didn't know, but it was too damn many.

"You two, get up that tree! Now!" Chief commanded, and then dropped to his knee to pull the magazine for his rifle from his backpack.

Matt didn't hesitate and ran to the nearest tree. The branches were low enough for him to get a firm handhold, and adrenalin had him climbing faster than he humanly thought possible.

Alex followed, but not quite with the speed that Matt had. The professor even cried out in pain as he pulled himself up. Aging muscles worked against the older man.

Once out of harm's way, Alex stood on a branch and leaned over as if trying to see past the leaves. "Natasha! Natasha!"

Chief had his rifle reloaded. He was on one knee and fired away. More grenades exploded, and Matt saw Chief launch his side rocket. It whistled a short distance before blowing a Troodon in half.

"Natasha! Natasha!" Alex cried out.

Son-of-a-bitch . . . motherfucking scum . . . murderer! Matt thought, feeling the rage rise into his face.

A wounded Troodon fell onto Chief, its deadly jaws clamping down on the poor man's head. Chief screamed for what seemed like a very long time. Other Troodons joined in the feast, biting arms and legs, ripping them from the torso. Some Troodons fought among themselves, playing a tug-of-war with body parts.

"Natasha! Natasha!" Alex droned on. He was on a branch below Matt, with his back turned.

Matt's eyes narrowed, and his upper lip raised showing teeth. Holding firmly to the branch, he lifted his right leg, and planted his foot square in the small of Alex's back.

The professor's grip slipped, and with a cry of surprise, he fell head first to the ground.

Three Troodons dashed over and began to eat the professor.

CHAPTER 18

Rifles spat muffled *pops*, grenades exploded sending Troodons' flesh and gore flying. Alex, Matt, and Chief had been isolated from the rest of the group. Natasha watched from behind Meat's large frame, too scared to pull out her own weapon.

The three Redwater crew stood side by side firing away. Logan joined in, had already emptied one magazine, and was deep into the other.

Natasha didn't know how many Troodons had been killed, or how many were left alive, for that matter.

Chief had yelled something, but she couldn't hear what. She did see Matt run to a tree and start climbing. Alex quickly followed, and both made it to safety.

At least she didn't need to worry about Alex right now. She looked around and didn't see any trees close by with branches low enough for her to reach.

"Them son-of-a-bitches keep coming!" Caveman said.

That was news Natasha didn't want to hear.

"Roll Tide, motherfucker!" Ron yelled, and launched a rocket. "Roll fucking Tide!"

The rocket's boom was quickly followed by the explosion of another rocket. Natasha had no idea how much ammo the Redwater's had used, she only hoped and prayed it would be enough.

Chief screamed. Natasha's knees threatened to turn to water. She tried to look but couldn't see past the line of men. There was no doubt the Troodons had the brave man in their deadly claws.

Alex steadily called her name. She could see the outline of his body in the tree but doubted he could see her. Poor Alex, he was probably worried sick about her. Natasha stepped a little to the side, raised her arm, and waved her hand.

Still, Alex called, that same apprehension in his tone that indicated he didn't see her.

And then she saw Alex fall from the tree, his cry brief before he smashed to the ground.

"Alex!" Natasha screamed, and darted past Logan toward her lover.

"Natasha!" Logan dropped his empty pistol and grabbed onto her arm. "Are you nuts? Get back here." He pulled her behind the line of mercenaries.

"Alex! Alex!" Natasha continued, and crumpled to the ground.

The professor wailed as the Troodons divided up his body parts.

"We got to pull back. There's still too many. We need to find a cave—something we can hide in and defend," Meat said.

"I'm going to hold them off. Y'all head on out," Caveman said, and then launched a grenade.

"Let's, go!" Logan grabbed Natasha by the hand.

She struggled to her feet, tears streaming down her face, and felt Logan pulling her along.

"Faster," Logan said.

"I'm trying." Natasha's head buzzed, shock had her not thinking straight. None of this seemed worth it. She wanted just to give up and die.

"Hold my rifle." Meat thrust his JNY-7 into Logan's other hand, grabbed Natasha by the waist, and threw her over his shoulder. "Let's go!"

Natasha watched Caveman run past Ron and follow them. Ron now took point and provided cover fire while they escaped. She imagined this was a designed maneuver they had learned from military experience.

These men were risking their lives to save her and Logan. They could have very well used them for bait while they escaped. That thought somehow sparked her will to live.

"Put me down. I'm okay. I can run," she said to Meat.

The big Samoan barreled around trees and past brush, and in midstride, pulled her off his shoulder and planted her feet on the ground. He reached back and took his rifle from Logan. "Go, go, go!"

Caveman ran toward Meat, who took a defensive stand. "I've got point."

At that time, Ron's rifle went silent, and his death cry chilled the air.

Natasha turned back and saw Meat give Caveman a hand signal to leave. The big man then backpedaled in a slow trot, keeping his rifle up and ready to fire.

Caveman couldn't have beaten her or Logan in a footrace, but the man moved at a decent clip.

"Hear that?" Logan asked.

The dull roar she had heard in the background didn't register until now.

"It's the waterfall. Let's head toward the water," Logan said.

"What about crocodiles?" Natasha asked.

Logan frowned and shook his head.

Yeah, they would worry about that if it came down to it. The only goal now was staying alive long enough to have a chance.

Meat's rifle popped off more rounds, and then a grenade exploded. After that, nothing.

The sound of the waterfall grew louder by the minute. The brushy area opened to a clearing leading to where she thought the water should be. Soon, the waterfall came into view, and they had arrived right where the creek spilled down tens of feet into a river below it. The earth ended at the river's edge. They essentially were on a cliff, maybe some 50 or 60 feet above the river. They could continue heading north along the edge, but if there were more Troodons than ammo left, traveling that way would do no good. She didn't know if they could survive the jump.

Natasha turned and saw Meat running toward them. Caveman had stopped 30 yards away and put a new magazine in his rifle. Meat was just about to him.

"I think I got 'em all," Meat called.

"Thank goodness," Natasha said.

"Yeah, I didn't want to jump down into that swirly mess," Logan said.

About that time Caveman lifted his rifle and began firing.

Meat looked behind him, but kept on running. "Oh shit. Caveman, come on, man."

"I'm right behind you," Caveman said. "Die, you bastards. Die!"

Meat turned and fired. His rifle cranked out two shots before something went wrong. "It's jammed!"

"Go on, get!" Caveman said while blasting away.

Meat climbed the gentle incline until he reached Natasha and Logan. He looked over the cliff's edge and crinkled his nose.

Caveman's rifle went silent. Four Troodons had surrounded him, and one had its mouth on his throat.

"Poor bastard," Meat said.

For the first time Natasha saw Meat's perpetual smile melt into sadness.

"We're next," Logan said.

"Can those things swim?" Meat asked.

"Yes, I'm pretty sure they can," Logan said.

Meat grunted. "Well then, let's hope they can't dive."

"But we don't know how deep it is. What if there're rocks?"

"I'll let you know." The big man turned and bounded off the edge of the cliff, holding his arms tightly around his rifle.

The two rushed to the edge and saw Meat hit the water, and then disappear from the surface.

"Clint. Oh, Clint," Natasha fretted. She just knew the worst had happened. What were the chances of the river being deep enough so close to the edge? She doubted there would be any crocodiles where the waterfall fell, but didn't know what other deadly unknowns might lurk about.

A head popped to the surface, followed by an arm steadily waving.

"He's okay!" Logan said. "You first, and then me."

Natasha looked over and saw the bloody mess of what was left of Caveman's body. It reminded her of a particularly gory dummy at a haunted house she'd seen. The carnivores had eaten so much it was indistinguishable from a human body and looked more like a slab of meat that would hang from a hook at a slaughterhouse.

One of the Troodons looked over at them and began his death stalk.

She turned to Logan, took a deep breath, and ran over the edge.

Natasha had jumped off the side of a cliff one time before during Spring Break, on a trip to Jamaica. She and her friends had paid a visit to the famous Rick's Café. Of course, she had downed enough rum to give her all the courage she needed to plunge 35 feet into the clear blue waters of the Gulf. Her stomach reached up to her throat then just as it did now, and her sphincter trembled a bit. When she splashed into the water then, she plunged so deep that her ears hurt from water pressure. Beyond that, the only negative thing she felt was the sting of impact on the soles of her feet. Oh, to be so lucky this time.

Her body hit the water, and she felt tiny needles prick all over her skin. This fall had definitely been longer than the Jamaica jump. Almost twice as long. As soon as she hit, she spread her legs, and poked out her arms. She didn't know how deep it was but wanted to do her best not to find out.

She came to the surface in time see Logan bail off the side and make his big splash. She turned her head and saw Meat about 30 yards away making a slow trek to the narrow bank that butted against the cliff's side.

Logan popped to the surface and lifted a thumb-up to indicate he was okay.

By some miracle, they had made it this far. She looked up to the cliff's edge, and at first thought she saw a Troodon staring down. It was only her imagination. Then her mind turned to Alex, and she remembered Chief's scream and Caveman's bloody body. Natasha shook the thoughts from her mind and made the swim toward Meat.

The big guy waited by the bank, with a hand out to help her. She reached up and felt his gentle grip, and she pulled herself out. "Thanks. That was some jump."

"The only time I've jumped that far before I had on a parachute," Meat said.

"You noticed how the river got shallower the farther away we went from the waterfall?" she said.

"Yeah. That's probably the only thing that saved us. The waterfall has eroded the river at that point. Had we jumped off a little ways from where we did, well, it wouldn't have been good," Meat said, and then grabbed onto Logan's hand as he swam up.

"Thanks," Logan said, and rubbed his back. "Could have landed better."

"Yeah, I bet my backside's redder than a baboon's ass," Meat said.

The three looked around. The river had carved out a 10 to 20 yard swath in the Earth. It didn't look like they could climb either side without the proper equipment. From their vantage point there were only two directions to go. South would lead past the waterfall and put them in the direction of the Warthog, but they would have to cross the river to do that. North would lead them, well, who knows? They needed to find a way back up.

"Our phones. We need to call Ben, and . . . Matt! Matt may still be alive," Natasha said.

"Yeah. He had made it into that tree. The Troodons shouldn't have been able to reach him. I . . . Natasha . . ." Logan said.

"Yes," she knew where her friend was going.

"Alex. I'm sorry about Alex."

She tried to hold back the tears, but one escaped. She wiped her cheek with her finger, and shook her head. "Me, too."

Logan wrapped his arms around her, and Meat placed his large hand on her shoulder.

Natasha pushed away, and cleared her throat. "Let's see about getting out of here. Try your phones."

Logan unclipped his and pushed the side button. "Shit. It's dead."

Natasha held the button in on hers hoping for better results. "Nothing."

"I forgot to turn mine on. Wait a minute," Meat said. The phone powered up with an electronic waking cry. He held his phone out for them to see. "I had mine in a protective case. It's a life saver when you fighting in war."

"Let me have it. I'm going to call Ben," Natasha said, and took the phone.

CHAPTER 19

Matt shook as he tightly clung to the tree branch. It was probably near 100 °F, but his face felt bitter numbness as if Artic winds blew against it. Beads of sweat formed on his brow and began to stream down his cheeks.

Chief was dead, ripped apart by the savage dinosaurs. The man only thought of his and Alex's safety during the attack. He had showed bravery to the end, and Matt felt awe for another human like he had never before.

There wasn't much left of Alex either. The Troodons had been quite efficient in devouring their kill. Matt thought back at the rage that had built inside—rage he never knew he was capable of feeling. He killed a man. Not some degenerate trying to do him harm, but an associate, a man well respected in the community, and yes, one of his dearest friends.

With fear and shock ruling his body now, he couldn't imagine how he ever brought himself to go through with the deed. It was as if something overruled his mind, took control of his body, as if he were just a spectator and watched his foot hit Alex in the back, and sending the man to a gruesome death. He had made himself judge, jury, and executioner. Would he be able to live with those thoughts for the rest of his life?

All the Troodons had gone. Those that had remained feeding on Chief and Alex didn't wait for him to come down from the tree. The Troodons followed after those who had gone after the rest of the group. Meat, Caveman, Ron . . . Logan and Natasha.

Strangely, when he thought of Logan and Natasha, he didn't know which one he felt the most concern for. Logan had been such a good friend—just a really great guy. Always giving and never really asking for anything in return. Matt hadn't met many people like that in life. Though he had a great attraction to Natasha, she had been stingy with her affections—hell, sometimes even common courtesy—giving him the cold shoulder and ignoring special things he had done for her. Yes, he did get that many of her actions were due to her relationship with Alex. But on this trip, he had made headway. He and Natasha had grown a lot closer—she had warmed up to his advances. It just wasn't by the way she spoke to him. Matt could see it in her eyes and in her expression. It . . . it was the same way she had been looking at Alex over the last couple of days.

Alex was gone, and if by some miracle the Redwater crew was able to defeat the Troodons and Natasha survive, he would be there to fill the void left in her heart.

It had been awhile since he heard the last grenade blast, even longer hearing the suppressed machine gun fire. How long? Time had become a blur. Was it 5 minutes or 5 hours? The event had distorted reality long enough.

He removed the satellite phone from his belt and dialed Ben.

The phone rang, Ben answered, "Go."

Matt went to speak, and the words refused to come out.

"Hello . . . Matt?"

This was ridiculous. Matt's lips quivered, and his face was so tight he didn't think he'd be able to form the words.

"Matt . . . Matt . . ."

"Yeah," he eked out.

"Hey. At first, I thought this was a butt call. What's up?" Ben asked.

"It's bad," Matt whispered. "Really bad."

The phone on Ben's end went silent.

He knew his friend's mind raced wildly right now considering the possibilities. He had to get it out. "There was an attack. Troodons. I don't know how many, but a lot." Matt looked around the area and figured there were at least 20 whole carcasses lying about. There were more, blown apart to varying degrees. "I only know that Chief and Alex are dead."

Ben gasped, and said, "No . . . Alex, no. Did . . . did . . ."

"Yeah. Troodons got him. Chief too."

"What about . . . what about the others?"

"They, uh, they were overwhelmed and retreated north. I don't know what happened to any of them. Maybe they found a place to hide," Matt said.

"No one else has called." The tone in Ben's voice showed he feared the worst.

"Maybe it's too soon. I didn't realize it until I turned on my phone, but this only started a little more than half hour ago. They might still be on the run."

"True. So, you need to get back here. Are you hurt in any way?" Ben asked.

"No. Alex and I climbed a tree during the attack. He . . . he was so worried about Natasha, he leaned too far out while trying to keep an eye on her and . . . and he just slipped and fell."

"Damn the luck," Ben said, and paused for a few moments. "I'm sorry, man, but I'm in no shape to come get you."

"I know, and I don't expect you to. I have two options, leave now before scavengers arrive to feed on the dead Troodons, or wait and see if the others survive and come back for me. I guess I need to roll the dice and just come back now," Matt said, his stomach quivering at the thought of leaving the safety of the tree and making the trip back to the Warthog alone.

"If it were me, I'd leave now," Ben said.

"Yeah. That's what I need to do."

"Look, I should call Coop and tell him, but I'm going to wait for you to get back first. I want you to leave your phone on for the trip back. I won't be able to help you if you get in trouble, but . . . but I want to know . . ."

"I understand. If the roles were reversed, I'd want to know if something bad happened—to have closure."

"Yeah, well, that's a polite way to put it," Ben said.

"Okay. I'm going put my phone on my belt and climb down the tree. I'll stay in voice contact along the way."

"Great. Matt?"

"Yeah?"

"Come back home to me, buddy."

"You know it," Matt said. He clipped his phone to his belt and carefully descended the tree.

He had to avoid a pile of shredded clothing and goo—that was Alex—at the base of the tree. It was hard to wrap his mind around the fact that was all that remained of a human he once knew.

Chief's body had been desecrated to the same extent. The mercenary's backpack had been torn during the feeding frenzy and the contents strewn about. Two hand grenades caught his interest.

He picked them up. The devices looked simple enough, if they worked like he'd seen in the movies. Hold the handle, pull the pin, release the grenade when ready, and hit the fucking dirt before it exploded. The two explosives clipped onto his belt.

Matt picked up Chief's rifle and held it across his chest. He hoped all he had to do is aim and pull the trigger, because beyond that, he didn't know how to operate the weapon. The area looked like a bloody battlefield, much like photos he'd seen from World War II.

A medium-sized pterosaur flew down from above and landed next to a dead Troodon. It began to eat, paying Matt no mind.

He knew more would come to enjoy the feast.

It was time to get the hell out of there.

*

"All right, guys. We're finally here," Coop said, and then powered down the Mule. "You are free to walk about."

The trip to the cave had been without any major incident. During the early part of yesterday, they saw many of the four-legged herd species of dinosaurs roaming about. Fortunately, the Mule either scared them from the path, or provided no interest. No other dinosaur had treated them as a threat, as the Triceratops had the previous day. On one hand it was a shame they killed the beast, but on the other, he grilled up as one fine steak. The meal would have been a bit more enjoyable had he paired it with a fine cabernet.

Coop got out of the Mule and massaged his buttocks, thankful he had a week or so before he'd have to make the trip again. The area was a bit in the wide open, but tree cover was close by. Nothing should be able to sneak up on them except, of course, something swooping down from above.

"Let's go to the cave and see if it's big enough to make camp there. It'd be easier to defend if we could," Coop said, and then his phone buzzed. He brought it to his ear, and answered, "Coop, here."

"It's Matt. I've got some bad news."

"Fuck, I don't like bad news," Coop whispered to himself. "What is it?"

"A little more than an hour ago . . . there was an attack. Chief and the Professor were killed."

Coop's heart sank. Chief was a man that had earned his respect many times over. "What got 'em?"

"Troodons."

"Okay, what the fuck are Troodons?" Coop was mad, mad at losing a friend. He couldn't hold the anger in.

"Bipedal theropod—about the size of a man. The guys killed most of them. There . . . there were just so many."

"So everyone else is okay? Put Ron on. I want to talk to him," Coop said.

Don had been unloading supplies from the rear. After Coop had said *Ron*, Don came around from the back and cast a wary gaze at Coop.

"Ron's not here. He's missing. Meat, Caveman, Natasha, Logan . . . we don't know where they are."

"Missing?" Coop said in an above normal level.

Don crept to Coop's side, turning his right ear as if to better hear the conversation. He then jerked the phone from his belt, touched the screen in rapid taps, and brought it to his ear.

Suge and Bats were on the other side of the Mule, staring intently Coop's way.

"The Troodons cut Chief, Alex, and me away from the others. Chief ordered Alex and me up a tree. They came so fast with so many that Chief didn't have a chance. Alex somehow fell out of the tree, and the Troodons were on him as soon as he hit the ground. The others had to fall back. I didn't see anyone die, but I did think I might have heard someone scream. I'm not sure."

Coop turned his gaze to Don, who slowly shook his head.

"Ben's making calls right now," Matt said. "Ben, any luck?" the associate professor's voice was slightly muffled. "He says no."

They had just arrived at the destination, and now this. Coop had to decide if he should complete the mission he was paid to do, or do the right thing and head back to the Warthog. He could take a vote, knowing what Don would say, but there was a large bonus waiting for every one if the trip ended successfully. If Ron, Caveman, and Meat were dead, it wouldn't serve any purpose to leave now. He couldn't bring them back. He—

"Wait! Ben's phone's ringing!" Matt said.

The surprised voice snapped him out of his funk.

"It's Natasha! She's alive!" Matt said, sounding happy and relieved at the same time. "Wait . . . Meat and Logan are alive, too."

Coop held his breath, waiting to hear more names.

"Hang on," Matt said.

Matt's and Ben's voices sounded distant, and Coop was not able to hear what was said. Whatever it was, he was certain the news wasn't good.

"Coop." Matt had returned to the phone. "I'm sorry to say that Ron and Caveman died saving the others."

"I see," Coop said. He looked over to Don, whose eyes pleaded for an answer. Coop lowered his gaze to the ground and bit his lip. Ron and Don had been together all their lives, most times acting as one individual rather than two separate people. This was going to be hard for Don to deal with.

Something inside Don must have told him that which he feared the most had come true. The poor man began to slowly walk in a circle, shifting from side to side on either foot while shaking his head. "Roll Tide," he told himself in a soft voice. "Roll Tide," he repeated over and over.

"What do we do now? Are you coming back?" Matt asked.

"I've got some thinking to do. First, tell Ben to hang up. I'm going to call Meat and find out what's going on. After that, I'll give you a call back. Is that clear?" Coop said, knowing it sounded more like an order than a request.

"Yes. We'll be right here waiting for your call," Matt said.

Coop ended the call, and was just about to step over to Don when a bone-chilling *SKEER-AK* sliced the air. He looked up and saw the biggest goddamned pterosaur he had ever imagined. The creature descended with the grace and speed he didn't think possible of such a huge creature.

A faint shadow grew larger around Don, and before anyone was able to react, two mighty claws had him by the shoulders and lifted him in the air.

"Don!" Coop yelled, close enough to feel the air from the flying reptile's wings and smell its funk. *Damn it!* They had all been so distracted by the call no one thought to be on the lookout.

Suge and Bats raced to the back of the Mule to get rifles.

Don's terror filled cries sent knives down Coop's spine. His friend was whisked away, and there was nothing he could do to help him.

Bats had his rifle up first and fired as the pterosaur quickly gained altitude.

"You'll hit Don!" Coop cried.

"That's not the worst thing that could happen to him right now," Bats said, and continued firing.

Suge had his rifle up and ready, but he too must have realized the futility of the situation.

The Pterosaur sailed out of sight, its destination the secret of the lost world of Patagonia.

"Damn it! Damn it to Hell! I bet that fucking lizard-bird was stalking us. That's probably the same one photographed here—the one that killed Prescott. It's learned how to hunt humans. I bet the longer man stays around the more aggressive these fucking dinosaurs will become," Coop said, and walked over to the Mule and pounded his fists on the hood.

"But Don—" Suge started.

"Don is fucking dead!" Coop yelled. "Ron is fucking dead," he said in a slightly calmer voice, and sighed.

Bats and Suge froze.

"Chief . . . John . . . too. Meat's the only one left alive," Coop said, sounding exhausted.

"Anyone else?" Suge asked.

"The young girl, Natasha. Matt, Ben, and Logan," Coop said.

"What happened?" Bats asked.

"Attacked by a bunch of two-legged meat eaters. Doesn't matter what they are." Coop slammed his fist on the Mule's hood two more times. "We let our guard down . . . lulled into thinking this place was some kind of fucking glorified petting zoo."

"So what are we going to do?" Suge asked.

Coop stood upright and composed himself, turned his head to the side, and said, "I'll tell you what we're going to do." He pointed to the cave. "We're going into that cave and find those damned diamonds. As soon as we do, we're getting the fuck out of here. We're too close just to leave, but I'll not risk anymore lives. Not even for all the money in the world."

He still needed to call Meat, find out where they were holed up, and make sure everyone was on the same page. Ben could drive the Warthog closer to their location. Beyond that, Meat and the two others would need to chance making a run to the Warthog. He saw no logic in sending Matt out to meet them. Coop touched the phone's screen and brought it to his ear.

As he raised his head and looked over at Suge and Bats, he first thought it was the wind rustling the tree branches behind them. Then a head poked through. A large crocodile-like head with a reptilian smile showing jagged sharp teeth slowly emerged.

The phone fell from his grasp, and at first all he could do was lift a hand and point.

His two companions must have seen the fear on his face. The two spun around as the creature bounded from the tree line.

"Dinosaur!" Coop shouted, and fumbled to pull his pistol from the side.

Bats threw his rifle down and jumped in the passenger's side of the Mule.

Suge ran to the side and brought up his rifle. He fired a few three round bursts from the machine gun and then launched a rocket.

The dinosaur roared as the missile hit its side and exploded. Though obviously hurt, it didn't slow much at all.

The Mule's .50 caliber lifted from the roof and zeroed in on the creature. The dinosaur was some type of giant theropod. When he saw the spines on its back, he remembered Alex telling him about the Spinosaurus. Alex said it was bigger than the T-rex, and this son-of-a-bitch was a monster!

Bullets zipped out the .50 cal., striking the dinosaur in the chest. Bats had kept his cool and gave them a chance to win. Coop felt like he had brought a Popsicle to a knife fight as he fired his weapon at the charging dinosaur.

The Spinosaurus slowed as it approached the Mule. Coop was amazed that the animal didn't immediately drop. Its chest was a shredded mess, and blood gushed out painting it red.

Despite Bats' best effort, the Spinosaurus turned as it reached the Mule and brought its tail around—slamming it across the side.

Suge ran for his life, and Coop backed toward the cave. The Mule rolled over and came to a rest with its wheels pointing to the sky.

The Spinosaurus raised its short arms in the air and let out a mighty roar. But then it lowered its head and began to sway from side to side. When it fell, the earth shook.

Coop saw Bats' bloody and misshapen face against the Mule's windshield. He wasn't sure, but the way the head cocked away from the shoulders, the man's neck must have broken.

"Look!" Suge yelled.

Two more Spinosauri burst through the woods. One headed straight for Suge, and the other came directly at Coop. There was only one way for him to run—and that was to the cave.

As he ran, he caught a glimpse over his shoulder of the Spinosaurus chasing Suge. It lowered its head and stretched out its neck, much like a goose on the attack. There was no way the man could outrun the savage dinosaur.

Coop ran into the mouth of the cave and stumbled on a backpack on the ground. He rolled on his side and saw a pouch laying in front of his face. He grabbed it and quickly sat up. He opened it to find the precious red diamonds, beautiful beyond dreams.

Suge screamed in the distance, snapping Coop to reality. And then the cave vibrated with a Spinosaurus' roar.

He turned and saw the massive body of the dinosaur overshadowing the cave's entrance. Its head slid in, and the eyes seemed to glow as red as the diamonds. Coop crawled away as fast as he could, praying the elongated head and neck wouldn't be able to reach him.

The dinosaur roared again. Coop felt its hot breath on the back of his neck. He didn't slow his escape and quickly disappeared into darkness, out of the creature's reach.

Coop turned and sat looking toward the mouth of the cave. He saw the outline of the head and parts of the neck. That was one scary looking beast. The dinosaur's head reminded him of pictures of dragons. Dragons weren't real, and these things shouldn't exist on Earth today.

Now what to do? Wait around and die of thirst or starvation? Surely one small human wouldn't be enough to keep this big guy around. Coop imagined a dinosaur that large would need to eat five to ten humans a day to get by.

The Spinosaurus seemed to be content to wait for now. A low rumble resembling a purr sounded from its throat. It breathed in short blasts, reminding Coop of a bellows shooting air over burning embers.

A *hiss* from behind forced out an ounce of urine. *Shit!* Something else was in the cave.

Coop sprang to his feet and tried to see through the darkness, but that was impossible. He realized he had dropped his pistol when he ran for the cave. All he had was his knife. With a shaky hand, he pulled it from its sheath.

Something moved his way. He heard what he imagined was a tail dragging on the ground. This was not good. He was trapped with nowhere to run.

The theropod leaped out from the darkness, forcing Coop into retreat. He stabbed at empty air in front of him, knowing he was forced to stand his ground and fight. The Spinosaurus' mouth was only a few feet away.

Fortunately, the theropod wasn't very large, only coming around waist high. But it did have sharp looking teeth and claws that he knew could do a lot of damage to flesh. This was a fight he needed to win.

After taking a deep breath, he held the knife by his side and brought it back, and then charged—bringing the knife up and plunging it in the dinosaur's chest.

It hissed again and bit down on the arm with the knife, shaking its head, and tearing flesh.

Coop screamed and instinctually struggled to pull himself away. His bicep ripping from his arm made a sickening sound, and he stumbled backward and fell to the ground.

As he rose to get away from the jaws of the Spinosaurus, something grabbed the back of his shirt collar. He watched his feet drag along the ground as he was pulled out the cave.

Coop was in the air now, hanging from the mouth of the Spinosaurus in front of the cave. He realized he still held onto the pouch of diamonds in his left hand. Pretty rocks that had cost Chief, Caveman, Ron, Don, and Suge their lives. They would cost him his life, too.

Coop felt gravity take control as the Spinosaurus dropped him to the ground. He hit hard, surely breaking bones.

The Spinosaurus lowered its wicked looking head and sniffed his body, and then placed a massive foot on his legs.

Great pain shot through him when the sharp teeth punctured his face and skull. For some reason he felt like he deserved this judgment. And as the final darkness overshadowed consciousness, he prayed for forgiveness.

CHAPTER 20

Ben's phone rang. It was in his hand. He looked at the screen and turned to Matt. "It's Meat's phone. I thought Coop would be calling us back."

Matt shrugged.

Ben answered, "Hey. Did Coop call you?"

"I think so," Meat said.

"It's Meat," Ben said to Matt. "What do you mean, *I think so?*"

"It was Coop's phone, but I didn't talk to anyone. My phone rang and I answered. No one was there, and then I started hearing gunfire. Then an explosion and a dinosaur cry. I knew then something big was up. The Mule's machine gun went into overdrive, and then I heard a loud crash before the phone went dead. I tried Bats, Suge, and Don. None of them answered."

Ben shook his head. "That doesn't sound good."

Matt rose from his seat and stood in front of Ben, waiting for the bad news.

"Given the circumstances, I'm going to call the shots. We're going to have to find our way out of here. We're heading north. If I read the map on my phone correctly, we only have a couple of miles to go before the terrain starts to change. Hopefully, we'll be able to find a way up. I want you guys to break down camp. Use the GPS tracking to get as close to our current location as you can. It's best if we limit communication in order for me conserve battery. In fact, I'll be turning my phone off until we find a way out and want you to come get us, or in six hours—whatever comes first. Sound like a plan?" Meat asked.

"As good as any," Ben said. "We're going to get busy breaking camp now. Tell Logan and Natasha we're praying for them. You, too, big guy. Be careful. You aren't going to get many second chances."

"Tell me about it," Meat said. "Signing off."

Ben ended the call. He turned his gaze to Matt, frowned, and shook his head. "Meat got a call from Coop's phone, but no one was on the other line. He heard weapons firing . . . and a dinosaur cry. That's it. The call dropped, and he tried the other phones, but no one answered."

"My God," Matt said, and sat back down. "What does Meat want us to do?"

"He wants us to pull up stakes and get closer to his location. They're going to find a way up. We'll meet with them."

"Well, I guess we don't have many other options. I'll get busy tearing down the canopy."

"Sorry, I'm not going to be much help. Leave the lights and stuff—anything else that's not essential. I'll man the machine gun remotely and keep an eye out for you. We don't need any more surprises," Ben said.

*

"Okay, let's take a quick inventory," Meat said. He fumbled with his rifle and detached the pistol/lower receiver. After leaning the rifle against the cliff's wall, he tried to unjam the gun.

Fortunately, all three of the survivors had maintained possession of their backpacks.

Logan saw that Natasha had her pistol in the holster, but his was missing. He had either dropped it while on the run or lost it in the water. "Let me have your gun," he said to Natasha.

She had her backpack in her hand and let it fall to the ground. With no protest, she pulled the .45 from its holster and handed it to him.

"Let me have your extra mag, too."

"I don't know what good these guns can do," she said.

"Ron was supposed to put extra ammo mags in all of your backpacks," Meat said, and then gave up on his pistol and tossed it aside. He removed his sidearm and placed it in the gap left in the rifle. It made a metallic *snap* when shoved into place. After racking the slide, he said, "There, good as new."

"That's a great design on that weapon. I wonder why other gun manufacturers haven't thought about interchangeable pistols and rifles," Logan said.

"Dunno. Probably some stupid international law treaty prevents it," Meat said.

"How much ammo do you have?" Logan asked while he examined the contents of his backpack. He had MREs, a medical kit, water purification tablets, but no ammo. "All I have is what Natasha gave me."

"I don't have any extra mags in my pack," Natasha said.

Meat had his bag open and shoved things around. "Nothing in my backpack except for two grenades." He took them and clipped them on his belt. "I might have thirty or forty rounds in my rifle."

"That's not very much," Natasha said, casting her gaze about, uncertainty gripping her expression.

"It'll have to be enough," Meat said. He rose and put the backpack over his shoulders. His red bandana was the only covering on his head—his cap a casualty of the jump.

"We're just out in the open. I feel so exposed," Logan said. The dry land between the river and the high walls of earth was only 10 to 15 feet wide. If something up ahead would make a charge for them, crossing the river would be the only escape. There was nothing immediately intimidating about the water. No raging currents or eddies to fear. No crocodiles sunning—waiting for something to eat, but what were the chances they could make it out of this unscathed?

"At least things are clear between here and that bend. According to the map, the terrain shifts just around it. That's our chance. We can be there in less than an hour."

"Okay, why don't you lead the way, Meat? Natasha, I want you in front of me. I'll keep an eye out behind us and on the river," Logan said.

"What about above? We haven't seen those giant pterosaurs yet, but we know they're here," Natasha said.

"Good thinking. We all need to keep that in mind," Meat said. "Y'all ready? Let's go."

The three walked at a steady pace heading north. The shore was mostly clay and didn't give much when stepped on, although, at times, did become a bit slippery.

For the better part of a half hour the three made the journey without speaking.

Logan was so focused on watching out for danger; he couldn't afford any other thoughts to distract him. They weren't that far away from making an escape. But even if safety were 10 feet away, one damn dinosaur could destroy all their hopes of survival.

"You know, Natasha, I've done a lot of reading in my downtime—a lot of thinking too—about what you said," Meat kept his focus forward as he spoke.

"Yeah, about what?" she asked.

"Shiva, Brahma—destruction, creation. I found a few websites while surfing my satellite phone dealing with Hinduism. Not only that, but I found somewhere they used physics and cosmology to show how the two belief systems matched. At first I thought it was a bit of a stretch, but then as I learned more, I started to see the point."

"There're actually several books written on the subject linking mysticism and quantum physics," Natasha said.

"Quantum physics, yeah. I've got to do a lot more reading before I can wrap my head around that. Anyway, I started thinking about life, about the universe—how it all began. I had read about Maya and thought about the big bang, and how the two could be the same thing," Meat said.

This was a bit of a surprise. Logan had never suspected a mercenary sidelining as a tattoo artist to be concerned with the deep mysteries of life. He had figured Meat more of the type who believed in UFOs and Bigfoot. The man had more character than he'd given him credit. Natasha must have noticed it, because she had been more familiar with Meat than any other of the Redwater crew.

Meat continued, "So, Maya is a Hindu belief that means: *the power that deludes*. I got to thinking, if there is a God, then what was life like for *Him* before creation? I mean, there's only God, and nothing else. This may sound stupid, but it sounds like a boring existence, although maybe it's stupid to think God can get bored. But, for whatever reason, the universe exploded into existence one day. The universe could be God's Maya. A delusion where God can escape being the all-knowing. He created the Earth and the Prakriti, which is kinda Hindu for *nature*. And God can hide in nature—become part of it, experience sensation unlike ever before. God can live in everything—germs, plants, animals, man. Everything." Meat stopped and turned around, they were just about to reach the bend. "I guess everyone asks the question '*Why are we here?*' at least once in their lifetime. That's the best explanation I can come up with right now."

"If . . . When we get out of here, we can talk some more about it," Natasha said, and placed her hand on his left arm.

"I'd like that," Meat said, his perpetual smile grew wider, and his eyes narrowed into little slits.

"The moment of truth has arrived," Logan said, worried of what monsters lurked on the other side waiting to devour them.

The three shimmied against the cliff wall and eased forward.

Meat raised a hand for them to stop and peered around the corner. After a few moments, he turned around. "Okay. I can see a way out of here. The problem is, there's a big mother of a Brontosaurus type dinosaur a couple of football fields from here. If we can get past it, the terrain inclines up at an angle and we should have no problem climbing out. Question is, what do we do?"

"We can hide here and wait for it to leave," Natasha said.

"We could, but what else may show up before it does? The sauropod may be huge, but it's a plant eater," Logan said, and lowered the pistol he had been carrying in the *ready position* from the onset. "I don't want to die, and I don't want to suggest anything to convince either of you to take a risk you don't want. I have this feeling that we need to keep going. Maybe if we move slowly enough we won't attract any attention. If we're going to vote, I vote we take our chances now. To be honest, the fucking suspense of '*Are we going to live or di*e?' is eating me up."

"Military protocol says in a hostile environment with no chance of rescue, the right thing to do is keep moving," Meat said. "Natasha, I vote we go, but if you say *no*, then I'll let your vote rule."

Natasha looked up at Meat, and then back to Logan.

Logan felt a bit slighted at the moment, but now wasn't the time to argue. He slowly nodded his head.

"I guess we should keep going," she finally said.

"Okay, stay close to the wall. If it's not looking our way we can go faster," Meat said. He pulled his canteen off his belt for a drink.

Logan and Natasha both did he same.

Meat gave the hand signal, and the three stepped around the bend.

*

The three had crept along the wall of earth without calling attention to the sauropod even once. The mighty beast had been content wading in the shallow water and munching on leaves in trees growing along the bank. Its rear side had faced them along the way, but they were about 30 yards away from coming up alongside of it. That damn dinosaur was as big as a medium sized two-story house. Logan was thankful it wasn't a meat eater.

Movement on the opposite bank caught Logan's gaze. He instantly froze at the sight. A group of Velociraptors had come to the river. "Guys," Logan whispered.

Natasha and Meat stopped and turned.

Logan nodded in the direction of the predators.

They both looked and saw the impending danger.

"Don't move," Meat whispered.

Good advice, Logan thought. No sense in calling any unwanted attraction. The Velociraptors were more than likely here for a drink. Hopefully, they would soon be on their way.

The small theropods, not quite the size of an average man, Logan thought, were evil looking bastards. His mind kept shifting to the portrayal of Velociraptors in the *Jurassic Park* movies. While not as large, he was sure they could be as deadly to humans. Especially with this many. He counted twelve in the flock.

The raptors stood by the edge of the water and drank, taking a mouthful of water and then throwing the head back to swallow, birdlike. Evolution had been kind to humanity. Logan couldn't imagine what life would be like if dinosaurs hadn't evolved into birds.

One raptor stopped drinking, put its nose in the air, and looked Logan's way.

Shit, he thought. This couldn't possibly be happening.

But it was.

The Velociraptor screeched out a cry and dove into the river. The others followed like ducklings after their mother.

"Run," Meat cried, holding his rifle in front of him in both hands.

Logan saw heads speed across the river like torpedoes. How was it those damn things swam that fast? Up ahead, the

Brachiosaurus passed an annoyed glance their way as they quickly approached. They would have to run past it before reaching the escape path.

Natasha slipped and fell face down.

Meat stopped, grabbed her hand, and helped lift her up.

The first raptor reached shallow water and headed for them.

Logan pointed his gun and fired two shots—missing the charging dinosaur.

Pap-pap, Meat's rifle spat, hitting the raptor in the chest and dropping it in its tracks.

"We're not going to make it!" Natasha cried.

Other raptors reached the shallow waters and sped their way. From the looks of things, Logan thought Natasha was right. They couldn't outrun them; they'd have to stand and fight. They needed shelter—a point to defend. *The Brachiosaurus!* he thought. It was crazy, but what other chance did they have?

"Run by the Brachiosaurus," Logan ordered.

"What?" Meat said.

"Let's use it to hide by. Come on!" This was no time for debate. Logan ran past Natasha and grabbed her hand, pulling her toward the sauropod.

Meat fired a few shots, and Logan saw another raptor fall.

Mercifully, the Brachiosaurus remained aloof of the situation. Was the thing that stupid or was it that they were too small for it to feel endangered? It didn't matter.

The three took refuge behind one of the back legs. The leg reminded Logan of a massive concrete column used to support bridges. He and Meat took steady aim, and began firing as the targets presented themselves.

The water slowed the raptors to give them a fighting chance. Logan thought he had hit at least two of the dinosaurs before his first magazine emptied. He reloaded and fired again.

Meat methodically fired shots, not every shot finding its mark.

Logan just now noticed the rifle's scope was missing—broken off in the jump, no doubt. When his pistol clicked empty, three raptors remained, fast approaching.

Meat pulled the trigger on his rifle, it fired, killing the predator—but the slide remained open. They were totally out of ammo now.

The three passed fearful looks, no doubt coming face to face with the inevitable.

And before the three attempted to make a futile run for safety, the large tail of the Brachiosaurus lifted into the air and smashed down on the approaching raptors—*cracking* the water with a thunderous sound and splashing it with a force that knocked all three of them over.

"Get up! Let's go." Meat was first to his feet and pulled Natasha and Logan both up, leaving the useless rifle behind.

The three ran north and started up the gentle incline by the bank of the river that led out of there. They were alive—saved by the ire of a giant. Logan's mind swirled as they slowly ascended to the top. If he did make it out of Patagonia alive, no one would ever believe a tale as fantastic as this.

When they reached the top, all three collapsed to the ground, with chests' heaving.

"We made it," Natasha said softly. "We made it."

Logan closed his eyes and felt the grass underneath his palms. The air still had the slight sulphur odor, but a fresh earthiness dominated. He cast a weary glance about, thinking he should be watching for the next hidden danger. For some reason, he knew there wasn't anything to fear. Maybe he was just too mentally and physically exhausted to care. Regardless, the Warthog couldn't be far away. They needed to get to it as soon as possible. "Meat, call Ben. It's time to go home."

*

Matt answered the phone before it finished its first ring. "Hey!"

"We made it. All of us. We're ready to come home," Meat said.

"Fan-fucking-tastic," Matt said. "Ben, you got their location on the GPS."

Ben gave him a thumb-up.

"You stay there. We'll get as close as we can," Matt said.

"Hold on," Ben called. "If we try to get even with them, there's about a two mile stretch for them to reach us. The woods are too thick, judging from the computer graph. If they hike south a half mile, we can get as close as a third of mile."

"You want to tell them?" Matt asked.

"Yeah, hand me the phone."

Matt rose from the bench and brought the phone to Ben, who still manned the machine gun and remote camera.

"Hey, I—"

"I heard. We need to travel south a ways, and then go east and meet up," Meat said.

"Yep. I'm going to send you the GPS target where you turn and head east, and where the Warthog will stage. We'll be waiting on you. It won't take us any time to get there," Ben said.

*

"We're going to backtrack south a bit before heading east. That's the closest the Warthog can make it to us. Y'all good to go?" Meat asked.

Natasha and Logan were both up and ready. The three traveled alongside the river, watching the terrain shift, and returned to the 60-foot separation between it and the ground they walked on.

No one said word. Their fast gait showed how eager they were to leave the place and join with Ben and Matt. *Matt, it would be so good to see Matt again*, Logan thought. Ben was a trooper and could take care of himself. Matt was a bit fragile, and needed all the support he could get from his friends.

The river below flowed slowly, and just as soon as Logan thought he could see and hear the waterfall, Meat's phone beeped.

"This is it. This is where we turn east. We'll be there in minutes."

Natasha's sweet smile melted as something rumbled through the trees in front of them.

Whatever it was, it was big.

The three froze as a T-rex emerged from the woods.

"Oh, hell no," Meat said. "I don't fucking believe it."

Logan noticed right from the start that this was the older Rex they had seen on the way up there. The aging one which had deformed ears and was probably deaf.

It sniffed the air and let out a roar that felt like electricity flowing through Logan's body.

"Back away," Meat said, and pointed.

"What—" Natasha started.

"Both of you back away. Now!" Meat shot them a glance hot enough to melt steel.

Logan put his hands on Natasha's shoulders and slowly backed up.

"You want some of this?" Meat walked away from them, staying close to the edge of the cliff. He took off his red bandana and twirled it in the air in front of him. "Come get me, you big pussy. I'm going to fuck you up."

"Clint, no!" Natasha cried.

The T-rex kept its beady, lifeless eyes on the mercenary, and after another fierce rage filled roar, stepped toward its kill.

"That's it, pussy. That's it." Meat let the bandana fall to the ground, and then he removed the two grenades from his belt. While holding them in either hand, he bit down on the pins, and pulled the grenades away. The pins fell from his mouth. "Come get my ass."

Logan watched the T-rex approach within striking distance. Meat's plan was obvious, and if it didn't work, the mercenary would never know. "Cover your ears," he told Natasha.

The old theropod leaned over to bite down on its prize.

Meat dropped the grenades to the ground, right near the feet of the beast.

Before the T-rex had the chance to sink its teeth into a soft human, the grenades exploded, the earth at the edge of the cliff gave way, and the heroic Samoan and beast tumbled off the side down to the river's edge.

"Clint! Clint," Natasha screamed as she ran and looked over the ledge.

Logan quickly came to her side and held her while she leaned over, her hands covered her face. "Oh, Clint. Clint!" She paused, and then said, "He died for us . . . He died for me."

Natasha turned, and Logan put his arms around her while she cried large tears onto his shoulder.

"It's going to be okay. It's going to be okay," Logan said.

"Matt . . . I need Matt," Natasha whispered through tears.

Logan gazed into the distance, his eyes narrowed, and his face tightened. "Natasha . . . Natasha, look! Clint's moving! He's alive."

Natasha spun around and looked over the ledge. "Where . . ."

One slight push was all it took to send Natasha over the edge of the cliff and to her certain death.

*

"Matt! Get out there. I see someone coming . . . it's Logan!" Ben yelled.

Matt sprang from his seat and almost tripped as he leaped for the door. He opened it and ran as fast as his feet would carry him.

Logan sped around some brush and sprinted straight to him.

Matt grabbed Logan by the arms. "Logan! I'm so glad you're safe. Logan, where's Natasha? Where's Natasha?"

Logan held his hand in the air as he momentarily caught his breath. "Attacked. We were attacked . . . right when we turned to head east. A T-rex—the old one we saw on the way up here. It must have followed us."

"What happened?" Matt's body wilted, and he brought a hand to the side of his face.

"It happened so fast. We . . . were near the edge of the cliff—the river some fifty or sixty feet below. The Rex was so blinded by rage it ran right at us. We tried to scatter. It barely missed me but slammed right into Meat and Natasha. They all went over the edge. There . . . there was nothing I could do." Logan lowered his head. "I'm sorry, Matt. I'm sorry."

The associate professor bit his lower lip and nodded. He closed one eye and winced in pain. Then, the tears began to flow.

"I'm sorry, Matt," Logan said softly. He moved closer and put his arms around the taller man.

Ben stepped over by the front cabin's door, leaning on one crutch.

Logan lifted his left hand and waved him away. "It's going to be okay, Matt." Logan put his cheek against Matt's. "I'm going to be with you—to help you get through this. I'll take care of you. I don't want you to hurt. I just want to make you happy . . . I've always just wanted to make you happy."

EPILOGUE

The volcano poked through the earth like the Devil's horn piercing flesh. An open mouth replaced the mountain's peak as if thumped away from the flick of a massive finger. The vent hole of Hell burped black smoke and toxic gases into the glowing orange sky. Near the base, hot lava pooled in crevices and bubbled like water in a slow boiling pot.

Eleven naked bodies stood frozen in time as if in worship to the towering monolith. None bore the scars of their recent deaths.

And behind the eleven humans, a huge spiral of smoke churned like a slow moving pinwheel. Blues, greens, and reds flashed and burned in ethereal light in the vortex.

The ground rumbled, and from one dark cloud above, a jagged bolt of lightning cracked the sky, to be swallowed by the volcano's mouth.

The unseen grip released the humans. At first, they acted as if in a daze. Then they became aware of themselves, and flexed extremities.

Alex was the first to speak. "Where are we?"

The others curiously looked about, and then focused on him.

"The volcano. We're north of where we were," Coop said.

"But how?" Natasha said. "Why?"

"I don't like this," Suge said.

"Me neither," Caveman said.

Ron and Don had their gazes glued on each other and remained silent.

"Chief, I watched you die," Alex said. "The Troodons and—"

"Alex, you died too," Natasha said.

"Bats, Don, Suge . . . you were all killed at the cave site," Coop said.

"No," Bats said, throwing his arms out. "No. This can't be happening. Dead is dead." He walked in a small circle—others quickly moved out of his path. "Dead is dead." A pool of red-hot lava with a candle like flame on top set a few steps away. Bats walked over to the edge of it, and hollered, "Dead is dead!" The man stepped into the molten rock and disappeared from sight.

No one cried out in surprise.

"Wait a minute. I died," Susan said, shifting her gaze to the ground. Then, she turned to Alex. "And you killed me." In a fit of rage, she ran up to her husband and viciously pushed him backward.

Alex stumbled and toppled into a lava pool just behind him.

"Look, over there," Chief said, and pointed.

Bats emerged from vortex, his body as fit as a few moments before.

"What's happening?" Natasha asked.

Alex appeared next and found a spot near the group—away from Susan.

"Shiva destroys and Brahma creates," Meat said.

"The hell you say?" Caveman said.

"This universe—our reality. It exists only through death and resurrection. The cells in our body are constantly born to replace those that die. Atoms and molecules constantly shift, altered by cosmic events and unseen laws of nature. Reality is unstable—illusory," Meat said, having everyone's attention.

"That doesn't explain this." Natasha waved a hand around.

Meat paused a moment. "The universe is one gigantic house. It contains billions of galaxies and is made up of even more stars. Can you imagine all the possible forms of life out there? It's staggering. So, what if this house is made up of rooms? The Earth is a room with life unique anywhere in the universe." Meat stopped and pointed at the spinning vortex. "That thing over there—it's some kind of time pool. It's acting like a closet in Earth's room. It has created a microcosm of the universe. For whatever reason, the universe didn't want to lose these prehistoric creatures to time. The universe wants to preserve it, maybe for God to experience sensation through them."

"You know," Alex begin, "some of that makes sense. The dinosaurs here, from what I can tell, there aren't enough numbers to sustain the herds for these millions of years. They should have dwindled out of existence long before man arrived."

"So the dinosaurs here live until they die, and then they are reborn?" Suge asked.

"I assume so," Meat said. "Just like we have been."

"But why us? Why, if the universe needs their precious ancient animals, do they need modern day humans?" Natasha asked.

"I'm not sure. Maybe God wants to experience more sensation through human and dinosaur conflicts."

"Is this Hell?" Bats asked.

"I suspect at times we'll think it is," Chief said.

"God must be some sick motherfucker to play games like this," Bats said.

"I don't look at it that way," Meat said. "I've come to realize that God is all in all, and that He hides *in* His creation. He hides in us, too. *We* are that God. But because we are housed in a body of flesh, we are deluded in to believing we are separate from everything else. If we didn't have that separation . . . that delusion . . . perhaps God would have no purpose. Perhaps God without a purpose would cease to exist."

A low roar slowly increased in volume, the earth vibrated, and the mountains began to sway.

*

"Fast, Ben faster!" Matt cried. "That last boulder almost hit us."

"I've got it floored now. We're just about clear. Just hold on for a few more minutes," Ben said, his hands tightly clutched around the Warthog's steering wheel.

"We're going the make it, Matt. I can feel it," Logan said.

"Son-of-a-bitch!" Matt said, and watched from a rear camera. "It looks like the pass is completely buried. There's no way we can ever go back there."

"Who would want to? Fuck that place," Ben said.

"The Warthog's not shaking anymore. The earthquake has stopped. We're going to make it. I told you so," Logan said.

Ben slowed the Warthog and brought it to a stop. He breathed a sigh of relief. "Thank goodness. The camp's only a couple of miles away. I hope we can leave by tonight."

Matt looked over at Logan and closed an eye. "Why were you so confident that we were going to make it?"

"I'm not sure. Something about Patagonia stirred an awaking in me. It's a feeling I can't really put into words," Logan said.

Ben's jaw dropped, and he shook a finger. "I kinda know what you're talking about. There was something strange about that place—besides the dinosaurs. A feeling—like you said. I didn't know who, if any of us, was going to die on this trip. I just thought I was going to make it. And if I made it, then whoever was with me would make it too."

Logan slightly lifted his head and peered down his nose. "My feeling was stronger. I knew we were going to live. It was meant to be."

"Maybe, maybe not," Matt said.

"No. It was meant to be. And now, and forever, it will always end that way." Logan's face relaxed, and he smiled.

The End

 SEVERED**PRESS**

CHECK OUT OTHER GREAT DINOSAUR THRILLERS

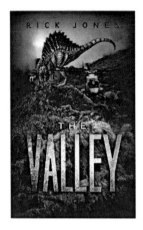

THE VALLEY
by Rick Jones

In a dystopian future, a self-contained valley in Argentina serves as the 'far arena' for those convicted of a crime. Inside the Valley: carnivorous dinosaurs generated from preserved DNA. The goal: cross the Valley to get to the Gates of Freedom. The chance of survival: no one has ever completed the journey. Convicted of crimes with little or no merit, Ben Peyton and others must battle their way across fields filled with the world's deadliest apex predators in order to reach salvation. All the while the journey is caught on cameras and broadcast to the world as a reality show, the deaths and killings real, the macabre appetite of the audience needing to be satiated as Ben Peyton leads his team to escape not only from a legal system that's more interested in entertainment than in justice, but also from the predators of the Valley.

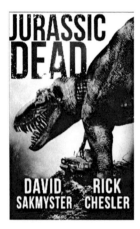

JURASSIC DEAD
by Rick Chesler & David Sakmyster

An Antarctic research team hoping to study microbial organisms in an underground lake discovers something far more amazing: perfectly preserved dinosaur corpses. After one thaws and wakes ravenously hungry, it becomes apparent that death, like life, will find a way.
Environmental activist Alex Ramirez, son of the expedition's paleontologist, came to Antarctica to defend the organisms from extinction, but soon learns that it is the human race that needs protecting.

CHECK OUT OTHER GREAT DINOSAUR THRILLERS

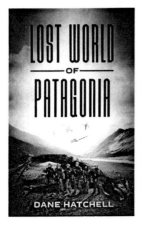

LOST WORLD OF PATAGONIA
by Dane Hatchell

An earthquake opens a path to a land hidden for millions of years. Under the guise of finding cryptid animals, Ace Corporation sends Alex Klasse, a Cryptozoologist and university professor, his associates, and a band of mercenaries to explore the Lost World of Patagonia. The crew boards a nuclear powered All-Terrain Tracked Carrier and takes a harrowing ride into the unknown.

The expedition soon discovers prehistoric creatures still exist. But the dangers won't prevent a sub-team from leaving the group in search of rare jewels. Tensions run high as personalities clash, and man proves to be just as deadly as the dinosaurs that roam the countryside.

Lost World of Patagonia is a prehistoric thriller filled with murder, mayhem, and savage dinosaur action.

SAVAGE ISLAND
by Alan Spencer

Somewhere in the Atlantic Ocean, an uncharted island has been used for the illegal dumping of chemicals and pollutants for years by Globo Corp's. Private investigator Pierce Range will learn plenty about the evil conglomerate when Susan Branch, an environmentalist from The Green Project, hires him to join the expedition to save her kidnapped father from Globo Corp's evil hands.

Things go to hell in a hurry once the team reaches the island. The bloodthirsty dinosaurs and voracious cannibals are only the beginning of the fight for survival. Pierce must unlock the mysteries surrounding the toxic operation and somehow remain in one piece to complete the rescue mission.

Ratchet up the body count, because this mission will leave the killing floor soaked in blood and chewed up corpses. When the insane battle ends, will there by anybody left alive to survive Savage Island?

CPSIA information can be obtained
at www.ICGtesting.com
Printed in the USA
LVOW12s1705160816

500618LV00009B/1071/P